FICTION RIVER: DARK AND DEADLY PASSIONS

An Original Anthology Magazine

EDITED BY KRISTINE KATHRYN RUSCH

Series editors
DEAN WESLEY SMITH & KRISTINE KATHRYN RUSCH

Fiction River: Dark and Deadly Passions
Copyright © 2021 by WMG Publishing
Published by WMG Publishing
Cover and layout copyright © 2021 by WMG Publishing
Editing and other written material copyright © 2021 by WMG Publishing
Cover art copyright © agsandrew/Depositphotos
Cover design by Allyson Longueira/WMG Publishing
ISBN-13: 978-1-56146-399-2
ISBN-10: 1-56146-399-x

"Introduction: Passions, Dark and Deadly" copyright © 2021 by Kristine Kathryn Rusch
"Some of This Is True" copyright © 2021 by Ron Collins
"Missing Carolyn" copyright © 2021 by Annie Reed
"Zero Tolerance" copyright © 2021 by Dayle A. Dermatis
"Lost and Found" copyright © 2021 by Laura Ware
"Tilting at Windmills" copyright © 2021 by Lauryn Christopher
"Not Getting Away With It" copyright © 2021 by Michael Warren Lucas
"With This Ring" copyright © 2021 by David Stier
"Twisted but Never Broken" copyright © 2021 by Rob Vagle
"What Breaks a Man" copyright © 2021 by Kari Kilgore
"Grief Spam" copyright © 2021 by Kristine Kathryn Rusch

This book is licensed for your personal enjoyment only. All rights reserved. This is a work of fiction. All characters and events portrayed in this book are fictional, and any resemblance to real people or incidents is purely coincidental. This book, or parts thereof, may not be reproduced in any form without permission.

CONTENTS

Introduction · v

SOME OF THIS IS TRUE · 1
Ron Collins

MISSING CAROLYN · 19
Annie Reed

ZERO TOLERANCE · 39
Dayle A. Dermatis

LOST AND FOUND · 55
Laura Ware

TILTING AT WINDMILLS · 79
Lauryn Christopher

NOT GETTING AWAY WITH IT · 95
Michael Warren Lucas

WITH THIS RING · 111
David Stier

TWISTED BUT NEVER BROKEN · 129
Rob Vagle

WHAT BREAKS A MAN · 149
Kari Kilgore

GRIEF SPAM · 167
Kristine Kathryn Rusch

About the Editor · 223

INTRODUCTION

Passions, Dark and Deadly

Somehow, as we got deep into our scheduling with WMG Publishing, our file headers for this project got shortened. The headers became "Passions," and I kinda skipped over it every time, figuring someone else had edited the volume, and I didn't remember the title.

Imagine my surprise when Allyson Longueira reminded me of my upcoming deadlines for the already-assembled *Passions*. Only...I couldn't imagine myself editing a volume of *Fiction River* called *Passions*. It sounds like a bad romance novel to me, or maybe an over-the-top telenovella.

I knew I had several half-finished volumes on my plate, mostly mystery and crime related. So I sat down to write a rather pointed email to Allyson when I realized that I should double-check the titles of the remaining volumes.

That's when I discovered *Dark and Deadly Passions*. And I breathed a sigh of relief. Because *that* sounds like—and *is*—a Kris anthology. I looked at the stories I had already bought, and remembered how marvelous each and every story was.

I remembered the *stories*, but not the title of the anthology. Which, to be fair, is not unusual. I've been known to forget the titles of my own novels and short stories. I always remember the act of writing them, and I remember what they're about. I just can't always

v

INTRODUCTION

recall what label I decided to slap on them, in the end. (Unless the title came first, which, for me, is rare.)

Dark and deadly passions fuel crime. And as those of you who read *Fiction River* regularly know, I adore crime stories.

What I wanted, when I sent out the call for this anthology, were stories about crime that came from emotion—often extreme emotion. I'm not a big fan of fiction about the bloodless intellectual puzzle-solving that so many mystery novels have devolved into. I don't like making murder a game, and I believe crime hurts its victims. So, playing at crime offends me on a deep level.

What that means for you is this: These stories are an emotional rollercoaster. A few of our revenge stories are lighter, because no one gets killed. But a light revenge story is almost a contradiction in terms. Still, in comparison to the other tales in the volume, these stories are almost upbeat.

We have some very dark stories here. Stories that will challenge you. Stories that will show you the underbelly of human nature. But, given who I am and what I like to read, there's always a bit of heroism—or an attempt to do the right thing.

We also have a warm story here, one that is a breather from the darker and more deadly stories in the volume. I must tell you that I *love* this story, and I put it in the middle to give you a respite from the swirling passions around it.

Not that this story is bloodless or passionless (well, it is bloodless. There is no blood in the story). It might have the most passion of all the stories. You'll see when you get there.

You're in for a treat. This volume has some of the best stories I've read in years.

Brace yourself for a swirl of emotions. Brace yourself for some dark and deadly passions.

—Kristine Kathryn Rusch
Las Vegas, NV
August 18, 2020

SOME OF THIS IS TRUE

RON COLLINS

This story is amazing. *I wondered, as I first read it, if it even belonged in a crime anthology. But the voice held me, and as the story progressed, I realized that yes, indeed, this belongs. In fact, this story is one of the highlights of an already-spectacular volume.*

Ron has contributed stories to many premier science fiction and fantasy publications, including Analog, Asimov's, and several issues of the Fiction River series. His short story "The White Game" from Fiction River: Hidden in Crime *was nominated for the Short Mystery Fiction Society's 2016 Derringer Award. He writes two series, Stealing the Sun, which is space-based science fiction, and Saga of the God-Touched Mage, which is fantasy. I think it's time he writes a crime series as well.*

We've only touched the surface of what Ron has done, so if you want to learn more, head to typosphere.com.

And as for this story, if I say much more, I'll spoil it. I'll just leave you to enjoy the ride.

It's dark as the car hurtles down the highway, maybe ten o'clock when *The Veldt* comes on the radio. It's a play about a family whose home has a room where you can imagine anything you want and make it become real. From the backseats, I look up and start to pay attention.

The car is a station wagon, a 1972 Galaxie, almost new.

It's big and yellow, with a black interior. Its engine is a throaty roar. Its tires beat against the concrete with a faded rhythm. Traffic is thin this time of night, just a few bright lights that come and go on the road. The radio is on a blurry AM channel that pops and flares with static. Everything smells like Mom's cigarettes and Dad's pipe.

My brother and I are in the "way-back"—a flat surface that only exists when we put the seats down. I'm fourteen, Kevin twelve. We're sprawled on our bellies with our feet pointing to the back. My thighs hurt because a metal rod runs across the seat where the fold doesn't quite disappear, and every time the car sways back or forth the rod presses hard against my muscles.

I'm holding three wooden dice in one hand and a flashlight in the other.

We've been playing a baseball game.

My team is the 1971 Oakland A's, which means the player sheets are only three years out of date. Kevin's got the Giants. It's the 7th inning and my A's are up 3-2, Blue Moon Odom on the mound with Willie McCovey coming to bat. There are two out. Tito Fuentes stands on second base.

The game sheets go dark when I flip the flashlight off.

"What you doing, kid?"

The voice comes from beside me.

It's a tiny man sitting cross-legged in a corner made by the door and the back of my dad's seat. Blue Moon Odom, the pitcher. His real name isn't Blue Moon, but everyone knows him that way. He's a thin guy with a rounded face that's too big for the rest of his body. He throws with an easy motion, the arm going up and down the slot in that effortless way talent has. He's got the whole kitchen sink, too. Now, though, Blue Moon Odom is as tiny as a leprechaun without the Irish. He's wearing pure white pants and a bright yellow pullover with a green "A's" on his chest. He points the glowing tip of the cigarette he's smoking at the scorecard we've left sitting in the dark.

"Game ain't over," he says.

"Later," I reply, shushing him.

"I don't think you understand," Blue Moon says. *"Game's not over."*

He grabs my arm and it's like my whole body gets a shot from the dentist.

Then I'm gone.

SOME OF THIS IS TRUE

Aside:

I don't usually think about vacations my family took when I was a kid.

Sometimes, though—say, like when I'm waiting for a meeting to start, or like this afternoon at lunch when my business cohort wanted to shoot the bull before getting to brass tacks—sometimes the topic comes up and I surprise myself by dredging out a five-year-old's memory of Kitty Hawk, or thoughts about when I was twelve and we did Mammoth Cave. We drove the Smoky Mountains once, brakes squealing as the car lurched over switchbacks and Mom sat white-knuckled and tersely repeating my dad's name over and over as he avoided crumbling shoulders and falling rock. Emergency lanes were mostly a concept back then. Guardrails optional.

Mostly what I remember of family travel is piling into the station wagon and taking I-65 from Louisville to South Bend, sitting in the back as the air's taste changed from sludgy mud into something cooler and filled with cornfields and cow manure.

When we were very young we would lean over the front seat as the car rocketed down the highway and watch for license plates from different states, or we'd peer out the windscreen and read billboards to find every letter in their proper order (oh, Burger Queen, how I miss you).

We must have made that trip a hundred thousand times.

Yeah, right, you're saying now. *A hundred thousand times! How'm I supposed to believe a damned thing you say when you spout something as hair-brained as that?*

I understand.

Maybe that was hyperbole, just me talking out my ass.

But, you know, it's strange what we can believe when we try.

Aside number two:

Family trees are strange. Where they start and where they end. For example, I can trace mine through Georgia, Ohio, and Illinois.

Or I can go farther out to Ireland, Scotland, and Germany. But when conversation turns to it, I say we're early American, farmers and tradesfolk. I've got people in the Civil War. Both sides, I'm sure.

Fact is, when I think of families I don't see trees at all.

Instead, I see it like we're all oceans, starting as a single drop of water at the top of a mountain, running to join with other drops until we gather enough force to become thin rivulets that fold into more and more flows to form bigger and bigger streams. We gather in tributaries and creeks, in bubbling brooks, and raging rivers, until finally every life you've ever touched becomes this big, churning body of water that is you.

Some streams you come on are pure, others fouled.

The most polluted are easier to avoid, but others hide their infections under surfaces that appear clean and glassy. The current moves forward though, only forward, and each stream you touch changes yours in ways you can't predict.

It's a theory, anyway.

The smell of popcorn and grass comes first, then the chill of damp air. It's a night game. Banks of flashlights cast shadows around the players, and the crowd rumbles with a wave of anticipation. My brother sits in the Giants dugout, but he's holding a transistor radio up to his ear and isn't paying attention.

Blue Moon and I stand on a deserted island out in the center of an ocean of green grass. He's tall, now. His right hand is huge and grips me by the shoulder, his other hand is covered by a brown mitt that holds a perfectly white baseball. The cigarette's gone, but I can smell it on his breath. McCovey stands at the left side of the plate, wagging a piece of lumber like a war club. Gene Tenace is behind the plate with his mask in his hand. His mustache is bushy and black.

I look to second, and Fuentes dives back to the bag.

The fans groan with impatience.

"*You got to roll the bones, man,*" Blue Moon says with a voice that sounds like it's coming out of a tunnel. *"Roll the bones or nothing happens."*

The dice are sharp and warm in my hand. I open my palm and they glow in the lights.

"Go on," Blue Moon says.

I close my fist and shake the cubes.

Aside:

Despite the fact that I carry his name, I didn't know my great uncle particularly well. This is why I didn't want to go to his funeral.

All right, that's not true.

If I'm going to do this, I need to do it straight, so let me say it for what it is: my desire to skip Uncle James's service wasn't that I didn't know him. It was that I didn't like him.

He was annoying.

I was fourteen, and the list of things I wanted to do more than go to his funeral was a million pages long and included things like getting punched by Tim Johnson.

I could stay at the house alone, I argued to my parents.

I could stay with friends.

Of course they made me go.

Here is the lump sum of my knowledge about Uncle James, though:

He ran a service station with my dad's dad. He liked movies. He wasn't married.

I don't remember thinking it was particularly strange that he wasn't married. I was a kid, and when you're a kid, you don't question certain things. That's just how it is.

James had been in the War.

He floated out in the Pacific with the rest of Our Boys as a radio communicator. Sometimes I could imagine him in a little gray compartment down in the bowels of a cruiser, tapping out codes while he wore a pair of brown headphones with padding cracking at the seams.

He ate lunch at a restaurant down the street from the station.

He was old.

He had wispy gray hair and an over-large gut, and when he came to family events, he was loud.

He drank martinis in an iced glass, a skewered olive always dangling in the corner.

He was obnoxious.

The word *obnoxious* sounds like a poison, doesn't it? Like anthrax, or arsenic. If you try hard enough you can hear a detective with a cigarette dangling from the corner of his mouth droning into a handheld phone from the other side of that same mouth. "The stiff died of an overdose of obnoxious," he would say.

If it was possible to say the wrong thing at the wrong time, Uncle James would say it.

The man could not shut up.

So he made me uncomfortable. I didn't want to go to his funeral.

I'm not fourteen anymore, though.

Now I see James was just an awkward old man whose life had flowed past him. Now I don't think James was obnoxious at all.

Instead I think he was just intensely alone.

I roll the dice.

The black one comes up a three, the white ones land on a zero and a three. I multiply the black one by ten, and add the white ones.

"Thirty-three," I say.

That's how the game works: roll the dice, then check the player sheets to find out what happens.

Blue Moon toes the rubber and peers in for the sign.

Tenace puts down two fingers, then pounds his glove, takes his set, and waits for Odom to throw that looping curveball he's got.

SOME OF THIS IS TRUE

It's a thing of beauty, arcing through space on a big, bending trajectory that's loopier than a smile from Richard Nixon.

The crack of the bat is all I need to know that McCovey gets it all, but still I watch as the ball rides its majestic way up into the starless sky. When it comes down it's just a white pellet that disappears into the throngs of faceless people who roar with open throats.

"*Shit,*" Blue Moon says.

McCovey rounds the bases.

Giants 4, A's 3.

The windows are rolled up now. Rows of yellow lights flash by, each surrounded by clouds of moths. Mom and Dad are quiet in the front seat, and Kevin and I sit in the darkness as the radio crackles and pops.

The host says *The Veldt* was written by Ray Bradbury.

I'm more of an Asimov guy, but that's still cool.

Peter and Wendy, the kids of George and Lydia, have this amazing nursery that lets them imagine anything they want. They use it to make their own African veldt, complete with a blazing sun, saw grass, and lions. Strange things start to happen though, and pretty soon George and Lydia are worried about the lions, which are always off in the distance eating something, and they're worried about the whole idea of giving their kids a place where they can imagine anything into existence. They worry that it's changing Peter and Wendy. They worry that the kids love it so much they don't want to do anything except retreat into this imaginary world of their own making.

It's an interesting question, I think during a commercial break.

What would I do if I could imagine a perfect world of my own?

Where would I go?

How different would it be from this world I know?

What's going to happen to Peter and Wendy?

By now the radio signal is fading, though. Whenever the car gets to the bottom of each rolling hill, the voices are absorbed by deep clouds of sharp static. As the story enters its last act the noise is past where we would normally just turn the thing off, but no one wants to say anything because the story has taken a twist. A doctor has suggested turning the room off. The kids fought against that idea and lost, of course, because everyone knows that grownups lose their imagination as they get older.

My brother's brow furrows into ditches as second by second the station fades deeper into the night until it's obvious we won't get to hear the end.

Still, no one says to turn it off.

The kids are going into the room for one last time. We're ready to find out what happens when Peter and Wendy confront the ravenous lions. We all want to know how the story ends.

Finally, though, the static screeches to the timbre of a screaming crowd and my dad gives in. He flips the channel to music.

"That sucks," my brother says.

Mom turns around.

"I won't have that kind of language, Kevin."

When she gets herself settled back, Kevin gives me a cheesy grin in a passing headlight.

"Can we go back?" he asks. Kevin wants to turn the car around to find a place where the reception is good.

"You can't go back, Kev," Dad replies, in that sagely tone he always uses when he means no. "You can never go back."

I sigh and roll onto my side.

The dice are still in my hand, hot and moist with sweat. There's something different about them now, though. They feel lighter, like they're buzzing or alive somehow. It's too dark to see but I can feel where their hard edges have left ruts in the meat of my palm.

My brain is still running loops about Peter and Wendy.

If the parents didn't want the kids to make this up, why did they get the room for them in the first place? What were the lions about? How would the kids deal with not being allowed into their play land now that they knew they were going to be punished?

I really want to know.
But I think something inside me already does.

Aside:

Here's the thing.

This whole story happened the night we drove from South Bend to Louisville after James's funeral, except for the parts that happened at other times and in other places.

Some of it is even true.

I'm pretty certain of that.

"Are you okay?" Jenny says as she piles into the car and pulls her purple bag in behind her. She buckles the seatbelt around her waist.

She's fifteen.

Her hair is long, and falls down around her shoulders—the ends are dipped blond. I make it a point to pick her up from school no later than 5:00 every day, fifteen minutes after cheerleading ends.

"Yeah, I'm fine," I say. "How was practice?"

She shrugs. Her lips clasp together. She's wearing pink lipstick like the rest of the team, so it makes a vivid line. "Becky is still being a pain in the ass."

I glare at her language.

"It's the truth, Dad. You always say to tell the truth."

I grimace and put the car in gear.

She's got homework to do when we get home, so I send her off to finish it and while I get dinner going I put the Mets and Diamondbacks on the MLB channel: $150 a year for the premium package. Not too bad.

I like baseball because it never loses touch with what it is, and because it's got that timeless thing to it that makes you feel like, if you let yourself dream just a little bit, you can still manage to see Henry Aaron or the Babe out there playing.

Dinner isn't too hard.

I do my best to make real food: green beans, leftover chicken, and fresh salad with real stuff. I'm not exactly a top chef, but I manage.

While the rice is cooking I fix the sliding door that leads to the patio. It needs WD-40. Actually, it needs a new door, but there's no time or money for that right now, so I get a can and take care of it.

I get the door rolling right just as the rice cooker pops.

It makes me feel better. A simple chore done after a long day.

"Dinner!" I yell to Jenny.

On TV, David Wright grounds out to third.

"I have to get back home," I say to Blue Moon.

"*You think this is Alice in Wonderland?*" he shoots back.

I glare at him.

The crowd is anxious.

The dice are half-buried in the dirt around the mound where a rosin bag might be. There's a trench dug deep in front of the rubber where Blue Moon and Steve Stone, the Giants' pitcher, have been toeing it all game. Stone stays to the left. Odom is more a center-right kind of guy.

Bobby Bonds is next up.

I hate that.

Bonds should bat lead-off like he did in real life, but my brother always puts him behind McCovey.

"*You gonna roll the dice, or what?*" Blue Moon says, staring down at me. His height and the fact he's standing on that hill make him look like the rubber guy in the Fantastic Four.

"I want to go home," I say.

Blue Moon pulls off his glove and rubs up the ball as he walks around the mound.

SOME OF THIS IS TRUE

"Boy," he finally says. *"If you wanted to go home, you'd already be there."*

It's after dinner, and the kitchen smells of heated rice.

I spend ten minutes and considerable elbow grease scrubbing the counters, then deal with the dishes. The skillet is the hardest part, but it only takes a few minutes. The metal studs holding the handle to the base gleam as I store it back under the oven.

Jenny's in her room now, texting or Imaging, or whatever teenage girls do with their friends these days. I'm sure she's plugged into music from someplace. She needs her downtime, too. She likes being alone. Sometimes, when she thinks I'm not watching her, she dances. I'm pretty sure that when I'm not home she sings, too.

I'm not allowed to witness these, of course, so I don't.

I feel the rumble coming from her room, though, and if I close my eyes I can see her move as the floor pounds in a rhythm. There's a reason she's on the cheer squad. Jenny's always been a dancer. I imagine her bopping around in her room with her friends on the computer screen in their own rooms.

The world today is a strange thing.

So big, but so small.

Other parents—the mothers mostly—used to ask me what I did to protect my little girl from all the ugly crap out there. Do you check her messenger? they would ask. Read her texts? Do you block her social media?

"I talk to her," I would tell them. "She doesn't have a mom now, so I talk to her every night at dinner and we figure out what's good for her. She's a good girl," I tell them, "I trust her."

The stares I got back were daggers, but screw 'em.

They stopped asking after a while.

It's been two years since Izzy left us for the cocaine and the music and whatever else it was she loved more. Nothing to do about it now except talk and wait for the day our phone rings to tell us she's taken one hit too many.

Jenny's an only child, so she's always been mature for her age. She knows all about her mom.

Education, I think.

Teach your kid how big the world is, and they'll be able to deal with it.

This works for us, anyway.

That's what I'm thinking as I scrape bits of Jenny's dinner into a container and clean the plates. Mine is always clean, but Jenny is a teenage girl. It's all right. We'll have the rest tomorrow. I suppose I could put the plates in the dishwasher, but with just the two of us it takes a long time for the machine to fill up and it's just as easy to do them right away.

As I scrub, the Diamondbacks are hitting.

Paul Goldschmidt swings from the right side. The count is 3-2.

My workday begins to seep into my mind as I get to the utensils. I've got a team meeting tomorrow afternoon, so I should prepare tonight. The IT staff is asking for help with their personnel assessment. They're always such a pain in the ass, as Jenny would say.

When the dishes are put away, I make myself a drink and sit down in the recliner.

Vodka martini. One a night whether I need it or not. I take a sip.

It makes me think of Uncle James.

The glass clunks as I set it down on the end table that Izzy and I bought when we were first married. The air conditioner is pushing hard, which reminds me I need to change the filter.

The clock reads 9:18.

I've got to get up early enough to get Jenny's breakfast ready.

I put my head back on the recliner and close my eyes for just a second.

"*What you doing, kid?*" the voice says.

It's Blue Moon Odom.

"I'm serious," I say to him, "I've got to go home."

"*I'm serious, too. Roll the damned dice.*"
His voice is sharp enough that I pick them up and throw a 24. Blue Moon gives up a ringing double to Bobby Bonds.

I roll them again and Chris Speier singles Bonds home on a dribbler just past Dick Green at second base.

"*Chris Fucking Speier?*" Blue Moon says as he throws his glove to the ground and stomps around the mound. "*You gotta be kiddin' me.*"

Speier hit .235 that year. There's no reason he should bat sixth in the order, but my brother has that annoying habit of looking at the world in his own way.

"*Wait till next year?*" I say.

"*Screw next year.*"

Everyone says Blue Moon Odom is a rabble-rouser. They say the Athletics are a rowdy team full of dissention and clubhouse fights, and that he's in the middle of his share. I'm sure they're right, but, fact is, everything will work out for Blue Moon Odom in the end. He's going to get shot before next season, and he's got a lot of other problems to sort out ahead of him, but he's going to be all right. Eventually.

But right now he's got Ken Harrelson coming to the plate and a ghostly looking Dick Williams, the A's manager, climbing the dugout steps and motioning the bullpen to yank his ass in favor of Darold Knowles.

Blue Moon spins on me. Raw anger lights up his face and he towers above me with eyes so wild I feel it down in the middle of my chest.

"*You can't take me out!*" he says.

"I don't understand."

"*You're the one that rolled the dice wrong.*"

"Stop it," I say. "I don't like this anymore."

"*Stop what?*" Blue Moon replies. "*This is your game, asshole. You're the one making the decisions.*"

"I didn't do it on purpose."

"*Chris Fucking Speier?*"

He's scaring me now. I can't handle it. I turn and run.

"Don't you run from me!" he screams as he chases.

Knowles runs in from the bullpen, but no one's watching.

That's because they're laughing now.

All of them: the players, the coaches, the fans.

They're laughing at me as I run figure eights around Tenace and the umpire, Blue Moon chasing me the whole way. A guy in the front row spits his Cracker Jack all over the woman beside him. She's not happy, and throws the rest of the box at me as I run toward the stands. My brother is still trying to catch the last radio waves of *The Veldt*, but he's laughing too. The only people not laughing are me and Blue Moon Odom. We may be playing Keystone Kops, but I know for certain that if Blue Moon catches me he's going to kill me right here in the middle of my own Fairyland baseball world, and then I'll never know what happens to Peter and Wendy or George and Lydia.

Except that I know how it ends.

I've read the book by now, and I understand about dreams and reality, really I do. I understand danger as Blue Moon's footsteps pound the grass behind me and as I run down the first base side. And, yet...

His stride is longer than mine.

I smell cigarette breath hot on my neck, so I turn a crisp right, skinning my shin on the corner of the dugout wall as I tumble to the floor of a cement-block tunnel that leads to the locker room.

It's bright with sunshine here.

5:00, I think.

It's 5:00 and I'm getting Jenny. But Jenny isn't here, so I'm running with Blue Moon Odom down a tunnel that I recognize is the path along the high school gymnasium, and where the sun is setting on the horizon, its rays slicing down at that angle that says a crisp nighttime is coming along. My feet pound a rhythm like tires beating on highway seams.

The police are here.

"Stop him!" I scream as I race past a female officer. "Stop Blue Moon!"

"You can't go in there, sir," another officer says, reaching for me as I blow past him, too.

The door slams and I'm in a room full of cops.

Two of them stand in front of a locker with the door still padlocked.

The name "Jenny Mathis" is stenciled into the plate above it.

The door is one of those metal mesh things you can see into. Her jeans are still folded on the top shelf. Her Bat Girl shirt is hung on a hook, her school windbreaker on the rung beside it, and that purple book bag of hers is lumped down on the locker's floor.

I stand there, gasping for air as my lungs try to expel themselves from my chest.

"Have you seen her?" I ask the cop when I'm finally able to manage it—he's a big guy with a big gun, short black hair, and a trim mustache that reminds me of Keith Hernandez, the first baseman of the Mets from back in the day.

"I'm sorry," he says, taking me gently but firmly by the bicep. *"I need you to leave, sir."*

That's when I see the blood.

Red and pooling on the floor. Red and splattered across the locker door. Red and splotched across the benches and the towels and the discarded athletic tape in a way that could never be washed clean.

I open my eyes and see that it's 2:15 AM by the light of my cable box.

My drink is still there, ice melted. I take a sip anyway. The alcohol still burns my throat.

Baseball Tonight is playing on a loop.

The Mets won.

I rub my eyes, and for just a moment I remember the feral look on Izzy's face as she sat in the witness box at her trial. I hear the emptiness in her voice as she explains how the drugs changed her, I recall the dead distance that draped itself over me as she described the ultimatum she gave Jenny that day: Move in with her, or else.

Izzy had been a mistake, a die rolled wrong, a stream with its poison hidden so deep no one saw it until it was too late.

I don't say anything at all as three commentators talk about magic numbers and playoff contenders, but in that moment of waking my heart screams and my head pounds with a sense of *What the Fuck* that's bigger than a billion universes can ever contain.

I sit up and take the drink to the kitchen.

Another sip and I pour it down the sink, then get out the dish soap.

As I clean the glass, I remember being on my knees in front of Jenny's locker, scrubbing at the places where I can still see the blood, rubbing the paint until the metal shined through, then scrubbing harder.

It's still there, I think.

The blood is still there.

Then I dry the glass, and put it back into the cupboard.

I turn the TV off, and walk down the corridor past the door where Jenny should be sleeping, turning the lights off as I go.

Tomorrow I'll make her waffles. Toasted twice, flipped and rotated in between.

MISSING CAROLYN

ANNIE REED

The passion vibrates off the page in Annie Reed's "Missing Carolyn." In real life, the emotions Annie's dealing with here are overwhelming. In fiction, they're just breathtaking.

Annie excels at writing crime fiction. Her award-winning story "The Color of Guilt," chosen as one of The Best Crime and Mystery Stories of 2016, originally appeared in Fiction River: Hidden in Crime. In addition to Hidden in Crime, she has appeared in 22 volumes of Fiction River and in WMG Publishing's Pulphouse Magazine. Her short fiction has also found its way into our Holiday Spectacular and our Year of the Cat series.

She's the author of the Abby Maxon private eye and Cumberland mystery novels. Her lighter fare includes the Diz & Dee mysteries, a smart mix of fantasy, humor, and crime. Find out more at www.annie-reed.com.

About this story, she writes, "I've written about survivor trauma and guilt before, but this time around I wanted to focus on something darker...the overwhelming, unquenchable need to get even with a faceless, unknown stranger."

The house felt too big.

Alex still expected Carolyn to be there when he got home from work. His job took him into the city, an hour commute each way if the traffic cooperated, two if it didn't. She always beat him home even if she had to make a last-minute run to the bank or the post office. The difference between working for a high-powered law firm in the financial district and a dental office in the suburbs.

He'd installed a motion sensor light over the front door and another inside the entryway. Too little, too late, but at least the house wasn't dark when he keyed open the front door and stepped inside.

Cold and big and empty, yes, but not dark.

He should get a dog, someone at the office had said. Something to keep him company.

He'd heard the remark in passing. Watercooler gossip in the

breakroom from people who probably didn't know he was standing just beyond the door trying like hell to remember where he'd been going and what he was supposed to be doing.

The remark had stuck with him.

Get a dog. As if a dog could replace the woman he'd loved since he'd been a junior in high school. The woman he'd expected to grow old with. To travel the world with once they both retired. Wasn't that the American dream? Work hard, live responsibly, and put away enough money to enjoy your golden years with the one person you couldn't live without?

Welcome to the American nightmare.

Alex put his briefcase down on the tiled floor of his entryway next to the coatrack. The motion sensor's blue-white light made the gray tiles and the off-white walls in the entry look ghostly cold and uninviting.

Except for the faint creaks of the house settling in the chill of the night, the only sounds were his own breathing and the scrape of his shoes on the slate tiles. The house was still full of their furniture, but the motion sensor light didn't reach that far into the darkness. Except for the entryway table, he might as well have been standing in some stranger's abandoned home. A place someone had slapped a fresh coat of paint on and put back on the market in the hope of finally catching a good sale.

The house even smelled stale.

No enticing aromas coming from the kitchen with a promise of a comfortable evening filled with good food, fine wine, and sitting on the couch together in front of the fire after a long, hard day at work.

They'd never had kids—both of them were too busy—and except for every other Friday night when Carolyn came to the city after she got off work so they could treat themselves to a well-deserved night on the town, they spent most evenings cuddled up beneath a fleece throw Carolyn had bought at one of the stores in the mall all the Goth kids went to. Sometimes they made it to the bedroom, but sometimes they didn't. Carolyn called the nights they made love on the couch their "romance movie" nights.

He loved their romance movie nights.

She'd laughed when she'd told him how the pierced and wildly tattooed clerk had tried not to look shocked when the frumpy, middle-aged woman had shown up at the register to buy a fleece for one of the metal bands featured on the store's sound system.

Frumpy had been Carolyn's word for herself. To Alex, she had always been the beautiful woman he'd stood next to in front of all their friends and pledged to love and protect for the rest of their lives.

The fleece had caught her eye as she walked past the store in the mall. She'd bought it because she liked the art. She thought it was pretty.

The artwork featured a skeleton crawling out of a grave.

That was Carolyn, finding beauty in everything.

He'd thrown the fleece away. The company he'd hired to clean up the house had gotten the blood out, but he'd still smelled it. Saw clots of it on the skeleton's grinning face along with bits of things he didn't want to think about.

He flipped on the light switch next to the front door, and lights came on over the stairs in the upstairs hallway. Warm light instead of the motion sensor's ghostly blue-white light.

He clicked the motion sensors off with a remote and trudged up the steps, loosening his tie. He grabbed a beer from the small refrigerator in the upstairs utility room and took a long drink. He didn't turn on the flat screen television or the stereo in the bedroom, an expensive entertainment package they'd bought each other as a tenth wedding anniversary gift.

That had been fifteen years ago. They'd never thought about replacing any of the components. The things still worked, and they'd been saving up for retirement. The only things they'd really splurged on were the two Friday nights out every month and Carolyn's laptop. She bought herself a new one every year.

He could throw the whole thing out the window now and it wouldn't matter anymore. Carolyn had always been the music lover. The one who liked to watch movies before bed. He used to think he preferred silence, but he'd never really known what silence was until after Carolyn was gone.

The first night he'd come back to his empty, quiet house after the police had released the crime scene.

After he'd paid someone to clean away Carolyn's blood.

That had been silence. Total and absolute and unrelenting.

Alex showered like he did every night, then he put on black jeans and a black turtleneck. He took another beer from the fridge and a gun from the lockbox beneath the bed, then he went to sit in the dark on the landing halfway down the stairs to the first floor.

He sat in the dark in his quiet house like he did every night, beer in his left hand, gun in his right.

Waiting for the bastards to come back.

Home invasion, the police told him.

Burglary gone bad.

"Probably been watching your house for a while," the police said. "Knew your routine better than you did. Just didn't expect your wife to be home."

Carolyn had taken a rare sick day. The flu had been going around, and some parent had brought their sick kid in for dental work rather than reschedule. Kids were little germ factories. No matter how careful the dental assistants were with their own hygiene, someone inevitably got sick, and then the whole office got sick.

That Friday it had been Carolyn's turn. She'd even joked about it.

"Bring me home some Dairy Queen," was the last thing she would ever say to him.

She'd had a soft spot for soft serve.

Except he'd worked too late that Friday night to pick up Dairy Queen on his way home. His call to let Carolyn know he wouldn't be home until midnight had gone straight to her voicemail.

The police wouldn't tell him if she'd already been dead when he called. Maybe they wanted to spare his feelings.

MISSING CAROLYN

Or maybe they just didn't know.

She always parked her car in the garage. Alex parked his in the driveway. After Alex left for work, the place had looked deserted.

She must have fallen asleep on the couch beneath the fleece. Forgotten to turn on any lights in the house.

He wondered when she'd first heard them. When they broke the little window next to the front door to flip the latch on the deadbolt? Or when they'd kicked in the panels on the front door after they'd discovered that the deadbolt was keyed on both sides?

The front door had been made of natural oak, but the decorative panels had been inserts. It didn't take a martial artist to kick holes in the front door by kicking out a panel or two.

Carolyn hadn't tried to call 9-1-1. The police had found her cell phone on the kitchen counter next to a cold cup of tea.

At least Alex hadn't been the one to find her. He'd lost count of how many people had said that to him. "At least you were spared that."

That particular honor had gone to a pair of teenagers who'd been walking the neighborhood trying to sell coupon books for a high school fundraiser. They'd noticed the broken front door and called the police.

But not before they'd looked inside.

They probably regretted that decision for a long time.

Carolyn had been sprawled on the living room floor just beyond the entryway, the fleece blanket wrapped around her upper body, her blood soaked into the carpet from where her head had been bashed in.

The living room had been ransacked. A lamp with a crystal base Carolyn had inherited from her mother had been smashed on the fireplace hearth. Books, including a few signed first editions, had been pulled off a built-in bookshelf, one of the features that had sold them on the house. Pages had been ripped out of the books, and the bindings torn. Artwork that Carolyn had picked out had been pulled down off the walls, the frames trashed, the prints shredded. Knickknacks that Carolyn had collected during her teenage years had been grabbed off the mantel over the fireplace and thrown against the wall, bits of porcelain stuck in the carpet.

Random destruction.

The only things stolen had been her wallet, her laptop, and a tablet.

And Carolyn's life.

"They took easy things to turn into cash," the police told him. "Probably high, looking for an easy score."

At least Alex and Carolyn didn't have any guns in the house. He'd heard that comment a lot, too.

No, they didn't have any guns. Not then.

The police had dusted a few flat surfaces for fingerprints. They took his for comparison, and he assumed they took Carolyn's. Later. But after a month, they'd made no arrests.

After six weeks, he figured they never would.

After seven, he bought a gun.

And came up with a plan.

The first thing he did was to buy a new laptop.

He didn't need it. He never brought work home—that had been Carolyn. He never even turned the new laptop on. He just took it out of the box and put the empty box on top of his garbage can nearly a week before the garbage was scheduled for pickup.

He bought motion sensor lights he could turn on and off with a remote. He turned the sensors off every night as soon as he made it through the door and made sure he was the only one in the house.

He started parking his own car in the garage. He covered the broken window by the front door with cardboard and duct tape.

And he bought a gun.

He knew next to nothing about guns. He still didn't. He'd gone to a gun shop and bought one he could hold and load, point and shoot. A pistol, not a revolver.

Something that held more than six bullets.

MISSING CAROLYN

Something that didn't need to be registered.

Was this a great country or what?

A few days later he bought a new game system. Top of the line. No games, just the system. He unpacked it and put it on the bed in the guest bedroom. He leaned the empty box alongside his garbage can next to the empty computer box.

He hated video games. He'd played a few when he was a kid, but he sucked at them. He could never get the combination of buttons down right. His characters jumped when they should have punched, ran into walls when they should have been running at the bad guys. He always chose the wrong weapon to use against the monsters. He certainly wasn't going to put in the time to learn a new game now.

But if you were going fishing, you needed bait.

Alex had almost finished his beer when the doorbell rang.

He limited himself to two beers a night, the first to numb himself to the pain of coming home to the empty house he'd shared with Carolyn, the one true love of his life, and the second to give him the patience to wait.

But he hadn't put out bait to attract anyone who'd ring a doorbell.

Alex ignored it.

After a few moments, the doorbell rang again.

Then someone pounded on the door.

He'd replaced the broken oak door with another one almost exactly like it, complete with decorative panel inserts. Easy to bust out with the right kind of kick.

Easy to use as a weapon.

The bastards who'd broken into his house had used a kicked-out door panel to beat Carolyn to death. The police had found it next to her body, which had been wrapped in her fleece blanket with the artwork skeleton crawling out of a grave.

"Mr. Crawford, I know you're in there," came a voice from the other side of his locked front door. "Open up. Police."

The voice was female, the pounding on the door authoritative.

Alex stretched out his stiff legs and stood up. He walked down the dark stairs and turned on the motion sensor lights with the remote.

The dark-haired woman standing in the ghostly blue-white light on his front step wasn't dressed in a police uniform, but she had that compact air of authority he'd come to associate with the police ever since Carolyn's death.

"You have identification?" he asked anyway.

She showed him her badge—a gold detective's shield.

"Morrisey," she said, introducing herself. "May I come in?"

He backed away from the door, an unspoken invitation, and went to turn on a light in the living room.

"You always carry your gun in the house?" she asked as she closed the front door behind herself.

He'd forgotten he even still had it.

"Seemed like a wise idea," he said. "Given recent events." He lifted his nearly empty beer bottle. At least he still remembered he was carrying that. "Want a beer, or are you on duty?"

"No. And no."

He thought about getting himself another beer from the fridge in the kitchen and decided against it. Instead he plopped himself down on the couch where he and Carolyn used to snuggle in front of the fireplace and sometimes make love. The fireplace was gas, easy enough to light, but he didn't plan to ever turn it on again.

The cop—Morrisey—sat down in an easy chair off to one side of the couch and looked at him.

"You mind putting that down?" she asked him, nodding toward the gun.

He dropped the gun on the couch next to where he sat.

"You have anything to tell me?" he asked. "Anything about the case?"

He already knew the answer—nothing new; sorry, Mr. Crawford

—but lawyers were trained that was how to cross-examine a hostile witness. Never ask a question if you didn't already know the answer.

Morrisey leaned forward in the chair. "Want to tell me what the hell you're doing?" she asked, ignoring his questions.

"Not having a beer with you."

The response came out fast—glib and sarcastic—but he couldn't seem to help himself. Sometime over the last few weeks he'd quit thinking that the police were good guys out there busting their butts trying to find his wife's killers.

"You're carrying a gun inside your own house," she said. "Sitting in the dark by yourself on a Friday night." She glanced around the room. "I don't see your new game system anywhere. You have it upstairs? With your new laptop?"

Trash had been picked up two days ago. The laptop and game console boxes were landfill by now.

"You been spying on me?" he asked.

"We've had units in the neighborhood. They pay attention. But I'm guessing that's not the kind of attention you're hoping to attract."

He didn't say anything. That was another thing they taught you in law school—how to keep your mouth shut.

She leaned forward in the easy chair, elbows on her knees. "You're playing a dangerous game. I think you're smart enough to know that."

He looked toward the dark, empty fireplace.

He wasn't smart. If he'd been smart, he would have come home from work on time so he could bring his sick wife her Dairy Queen. So he could have turned on the lights in the house so the robbers—the killers—would know someone was home and pass his house right on by.

The hell of it was that the deal he'd stayed late that night to hammer out had been revised five times since then.

His work had been a waste.

The whole damn, sad, sorry mess had been a waste. He'd cancelled Carolyn's credit cards while he'd still been in shock that night, and the killers never had a chance to use them. She didn't carry much cash in her wallet, maybe forty dollars tops. Her laptop was worth maybe five hundred bucks, her tablet a couple hundred more.

That's was what her life had been worth. Less than eight hundred dollars. What he billed his clients for two hours' work.

"Are you going to find the people who killed my wife?" he asked the detective. "Give her justice?"

Give him peace?

Just one night of peace?

He wished he'd grabbed another beer before he sat down on the couch.

"We're doing our best," she said. "But you have to give us a chance. Don't go adding to the problem."

The problem.

This case hadn't been just a simple smash and grab. A woman had died. It was like no one remembered that.

He closed his eyes. The muscles of his jaw ached from holding back his temper.

"I'll keep that in mind," he said. "Will there be anything else?"

She didn't answer, and eventually he opened his eyes to look at her.

Her cop expression had softened. For the first time he noticed that her eyes were as dark as her hair.

"I feel for you, Mr. Crawford," she said. "You might not believe that, but I do. You might not think we're trying to find your wife's killers, but we are. Junkies, meth heads, tweakers—one thing they all have in common is that they're stupid. They mess up. All they care about is their next score and they don't care what they have to do to get that. Eventually they screw up, and we'll be there to catch them. I want you to be alive when we do."

She stared at him for a long moment, and he thought she was going to say something like *your wife would want you alive, too,* but she surprised him. She simply got up from the chair and let herself out the front door without another word.

MISSING CAROLYN

She dropped a business card on the table by the front door before she left.

He didn't have the heart to go back to sitting on the landing in the dark. His heart ached in a way he wouldn't have thought possible only a few months ago.

He took out his cell phone to look at the time—not quite ten at night—but his eyes strayed to his voicemail icon. He thumbed it on. Pushed "play" on the last voicemail from his wife and put the phone to his ear.

He listened while she talked about a small frustration at work. Not really the reason for her call, she said. She wanted to let him know she'd be stopping by the store on her way home, did he want her to pick up anything special for dinner?

Her voice had been cheerful, the message nothing special. Just the type of message that married people left for each other. But now it was everything special. It was the only voicemail message she'd left him that he hadn't deleted before she'd been killed. Now he wished that he'd saved every single one.

He closed his eyes as he listened to the message again. And again. And five more times before he finally made himself stop.

Before he went up to bed he got another beer from the kitchen refrigerator. The remnants of last night's takeout sat in sad little boxes on the top shelf of the fridge. He thought about eating leftover chow mein, then closed the refrigerator door and went upstairs to bed.

He never heard the burglars break into his house until they were already through his new front door.

He should have stopped at two beers.

Three beers on an empty stomach and an empty, shattered heart had been too much. He'd fallen into a deep, dreamless sleep. He didn't hear anything until the fourth stair from the top creaked under a stealthy footfall.

He'd told Carolyn he would fix the creak if she wanted, but she'd said that was her early warning system for those nights when he was working late.

"So I can give my man-on-the-side time to hide in the closet," she'd said.

An old joke between the two of them. Her "man on the side" and his "girl at the office." Their version of "the list"—celebrities they were each allowed to sleep with, as if the occasion would ever arise.

He'd been so in love with her the thought had never even occurred to him that he might find someone else attractive. Even now—especially now—he couldn't imagine sharing his life with anyone ever again.

The stair creaked, and he snapped awake.

Listened for the sound to come again as the intruder's foot lifted from the step.

After a moment, it did.

The hair on the back of his neck stood on end. He wasn't alone in the house.

He never once thought it was Carolyn, back from the grave like the skeleton on the fleece blanket he'd thrown away. He didn't believe in ghosts. He didn't believe in the walking dead or demons or monsters.

Except monsters of the human variety. The kind of monsters who'd kill a sick woman in her own house just because she'd been in the way.

He reached for his gun. He always kept it on the bed next to him in the spot that had been Carolyn's. He still only slept on his side of the bed.

The gun wasn't there.

Of course, not. He'd left his gun on the couch. Forgotten it when he'd grabbed the third beer from the kitchen.

His head felt fuzzy, half stuffed with cotton, but his heart was beating double time.

He didn't have a weapon. He didn't have a way to fight back.

But he damn well sure wasn't going to be caught in his bed. Killed with a blanket wrapped around his head.

He slid from beneath the covers onto the bedroom floor and counted.

The squeaky riser was the fourth from the top.

The intruder would be careful now, waiting for another stair to creak. None of them did, but the intruder wouldn't know that. The police didn't think the robbers who'd killed Carolyn had made it upstairs. None of her jewelry had been taken. Alex had gambled on the assumption that the killers would come back to steal what they had missed.

The gamble had paid off, but he'd gone to bed unprepared.

He counted down from four slowly, imagining he was the killer on the stairs, placing each foot down easy, not sure if anyone was in the house. The cop—the detective—hadn't been here long. The killers could have missed her. Assumed that Alex no longer lived here since the house was always dark.

Alex scuttled across the bedroom floor, moving as quietly as he could, headed toward the entertainment center. Carolyn loved watching movies in bed, but their equipment had been old. Their Blu-ray player had been top of the line when they bought it, nearly the size of an old VCR with a heavy metal case. Carolyn had been talking about replacing it with a model that would let her stream some of the online services, but she hadn't done that yet.

He reached around the back of the Blu-ray player and pulled out all the wires, then lifted the heavy box up and held it two-handed over one shoulder like a baseball bat. He crept to one side of his bedroom door.

And then he waited.

His eyes were well adjusted to the dark. All those nights spent sitting in the dark on his stairs waiting for a moment just like this.

The burglar—the killer—took his time getting to the master bedroom. Alex heard the sound of wires rubbing on plastic, and then the rustle of cloth. The burglar must have gone into the guest bedroom first and found the unhooked game system. Probably slid it into a loot bag.

Easy money, boys. Go ahead and take the bait.

After a few more minutes, Alex finally saw movement at his bedroom door.

A gun—maybe his gun—followed by the hand and then the arm of the man sneaking into the master bedroom.

Alex made himself wait until the burglar—the killer—was through the doorway and Alex had a clear shot at the man's head.

He was a piss-poor excuse for a burglar (killer). He didn't even check the sides of the door.

Alex swung his wife's old Blu-ray player like a major league hitter aiming for the fences.

He hit the man square in the back of his head.

The impact sent numbing pain up Alex's arms all the way to his shoulders, and he nearly dropped the player.

The man dropped like a sack of cement on the bedroom carpet.

Alex hit him again. And again.

And again.

He was about ready to swing for the fifth time when he heard footsteps pounding up the stairs.

The burglar—the killer—wasn't alone.

Of course not. The police thought there'd been more than one killer in his house.

And if one of them were armed, both of them were armed. A dented Blu-ray player wasn't good enough against a killer who knew Alex was there.

He dropped the Blu-ray player and scrambled for the gun the burglar had dropped when Alex hit him.

His fingers closed around it the same time the other burglar (killer) burst through the bedroom door, gun arm extended in front of himself.

And tripped over the burglar Alex had brained with the Blu-ray player.

The burglar's shot went wide.

Alex fired the gun—his gun—over and over again until it clicked empty.

The second burglar dropped beside the first.

Neither man moved. Alex listened for any other sounds coming from downstairs, but his house was quiet again. Somewhere in the neighborhood a dog started barking.

They'd never had a dog. Never had any pets. Carolyn liked animals a lot, and it broke her heart that she couldn't have any, but her allergies wouldn't allow it.

Alex crossed his bedroom floor to the nightstand, careful not to step in any blood. He took his cell phone off the charger and called the police.

"I want to report a break-in," he said.

He was on hold when the shakes hit, and for the first time since the night Carolyn died, he started to cry.

This time Alex had to go to the station to give a statement. One of the other lawyers from the firm accompanied him just in case the questions got too intense, too pointed, but while the police didn't treat him gently, they treated him with respect.

The detective who took his statement wasn't Morrisey but a tired-looking, overweight man a few years short of retirement. He took Alex and his attorney into an interview room barely large enough for the three of them and the industrial gray desk and chairs. No art on the cinderblock walls, no one-way mirror, no discrete recording equipment. The detective used an app on his phone to record Alex's statement.

When the interview was over, the detective gave Alex a hard look.

"You're a lucky man," he said. "These two have been hitting houses all over the area. They're pros. Two-strike losers who've done hard time. They usually pick empty places filled with high-tech toys."

The detective paused, waiting for Alex to say something, but Alex knew better. He was a lawyer. He could out-wait anybody.

"Guess they figured out you'd bought some new stuff," the detective eventually said.

Alex shrugged. It had been a long night, and it would be a long day. He had things he had to do. Replacing his front door wasn't one of them.

He hadn't heard the burglars break in the night before because they'd used a gadget to pick his lock. Apparently it was the same kind of tool law enforcement agencies used when they wanted to disable a lock without breaking down the door.

They hadn't kicked in his front door.

They hadn't been the same killers who beat Carolyn to death for the money in her purse and her laptop and her tablet.

The men who'd broken into his house the night before wouldn't be breaking into anyone else's house. Alex had killed the man he'd shot. The other man would be in the hospital for a long time, but he'd probably never know it. Alex had caved in the side of the man's skull with Carolyn's old Blu-ray player.

"Guess you're gonna need something new to play your movies," the detective said.

"I don't watch movies," Alex said. "That was my wife."

The detective knew about Carolyn. Her death and the prior break-in was part of the official statement.

"I'm real sorry about what happened to your wife," the detective said. "You probably weren't thinking straight when you bought your new stuff, but it's wise to break the boxes up and stuff them in the can. Better still if you do that the same day the trash is picked up. The bad guys tend to notice stuff like that. Guess you could say it's their job."

Alex closed his eyes as a wave of weariness passed over him.

He'd taken care of the men who'd broken into his house, but he hadn't taken care of the men who'd killed Carolyn. They were still out there. Still getting high and stealing what didn't belong to them and taking lives with no more thought than where their next fix was coming from.

"I'll be more careful," Alex said. "Guess I didn't think things through."

The detective stood up and shook Alex's hand. "We'll be in touch if we need anything."

Alex thanked the lawyer from his firm as they parted ways on the steps in front of the police station. The sun was just cresting the mountains to the east. Another brand-new day with only a hint of clouds overhead.

Carolyn used to love watching the sun rise. Sit at the kitchen table and have a cup of tea and read a chapter or two of a novel on her tablet. She didn't have to be at work until nine, but she got up every morning so that she could kiss Alex goodbye as he left for work. He only saw the sunrise in his rearview mirror as he navigated heavy traffic into the city.

Another wave of loss washed over him, this one so strong that it took his breath away. He had to actually concentrate on breathing.

Carolyn would never get to see another sunrise. Never hold him in her arms and give him a kiss and tell him to go get the bad guys.

She meant on behalf of his clients, but he could still hear her words clear as day. Ever since her death, those words had taken on new meaning.

If he couldn't get the bad guys on behalf of his wife, what good was he?

He straightened his shoulders and scrubbed at his face. The lawyer from work had offered to give Alex a ride wherever he wanted to go—his house was a crime scene again—but Alex told the man he'd make his own way to the hotel he'd stayed at last time. He wanted time alone to think.

He had planning to do.

He had a new game system to buy. The other one he'd bought was now evidence.

So was his gun. He'd have to buy a new one.

Maybe more than one. He needed a gun he could leave upstairs all the time.

And another tablet. A high-end one that came in a big box. He'd have to research which one was considered the best.

Which model was the easiest to turn into quick cash.

He was still making plans when he heard someone call his name. A woman's voice.

He turned around to see Detective Morrisey coming down the stairs toward him.

"Detective," he said.

"I just read your statement," she said.

He kept his face carefully neutral. "I didn't know you were assigned to the case."

"They're related. I got copied." She gave him a hard look. "I get copied on anything that relates to you or to your wife's death."

He nodded. "That helps you catch who killed her?"

"We're working on it."

He hadn't expected anything different or he wouldn't have asked the question.

He started to turn away when she called his name again.

"You might want to consider a new hobby," she said. "This happens again, we might look at you a little harder. You're a lawyer. You know we can charge you."

He didn't say anything.

"Find something else to take up your time," she said. "Something you can care for besides yourself. Get a dog. They need a lot of attention. Help get you out of your head."

He allowed himself a small smile that he was sure didn't reach his eyes.

"Can't," he said. "My wife's allergic."

ZERO TOLERANCE

DAYLE A. DERMATIS

Dayle A. Dermatis has the rare gift of character. Her characters—particularly her series characters—are exceedingly memorable. You'll find many of them in her short fiction. She's published more than 100 short stories in multiple genres, appearing in such venues as Fiction River *(twenty-two volumes to date, most recently* Special Edition: Summer Sizzles, Superstitious, *and* Chances), Alfred Hitchcock's Mystery Magazine, *and* DAW Books.

For more information about her and her wonderful fiction, visit DayleDermatis.com, sign up for her newsletter, and/or support her on Patreon.

This story features one of Dayle's recurring characters, Brittani, a band geek who "cares too much about people she shouldn't." Stories about Brittani have appeared in our sister publication, Pulphouse Magazine, *and* Alfred Hitchcock's Mystery Magazine *has published a story featuring Brittani's grandmother.*

You don't have to have read any of these stories to enjoy "Zero Tolerance." I guarantee that you'll want to read them all after you've finished this one.

I'm not a writer, but there seem to be certain sounds that have no adequate description.

When you accidentally bite the inside of your lower lip, not just a catch, but when your front teeth actually crunch through the flesh, and you can hear it inside your head a split second before the pain hits.

The whisper-release of air from the lungs of someone who's just died, making you raise your head in hope...but no.

And—this one was a first for me, right now—the surprisingly solid yet somehow squishy thud of a fist connecting with a jaw.

Thankfully I was attached to neither the fist nor the jaw in question.

I had been tutoring freshman Steve Schotz on the third chair French horn part in the Wagner piece the band would be performing in the spring concert. It was a Thursday afternoon, and Mr. Wilke, the band director, had gone home. I help him out enough that he finally gave me a key to the band room, M102.

Steve had headed out of the room ahead of me, while I put the music stands away and prepared to lock up.

That was when I heard, from the hallway, "Well, if it isn't the faggot," which made me see fifty shades of red rage, and then I heard the punch.

The sound reverberated down the mostly empty high school back hallway as I ran. "Hey! *Oi!*"

(I don't know why I went British there for a moment.)

In my school, I'm known as The Fixer. Eyeroll on the name, which gives you an idea of the general creativity level of the student body. Normally my fixing involves figuring out how to get someone out of a stupid situation they've gotten themselves into.

Unless they've done something illegal. Then they're on their own.

At any rate, I'm not the type to wade into fights, even if I am almost six feet of boobs and sarcasm. I'd rather smart my way out of a situation. Also, I'm not terribly coordinated. I don't know if my parents named me Brittani-with-an-i because they were hoping for a delicate princess, but despite my height, neither modeling nor basketball are in my future. I like math, science, and music.

Which gives you a window into my popularity level—at least before I started fixing things for people.

It was three against one, the three being boys I didn't recognize; my guess was juniors, like me, or seniors. I had no fighting experience except for a self-defense course I took a few years ago, but I was taller than two of the boys, and at least the odds would be better.

The three had glanced up when I yelled, but one—Ryan Somebody, I thought—had Steve by the collar and there wasn't enough of a pause for Steve to wriggle free.

"Too bad you're too gay to have a girlfriend, faggot," Ryan sneered. "Otherwise she'd have to rescue you."

One of the other boys punched Steve in the stomach. He doubled over, and now Ryan either lost his grip or let go.

I didn't think; I acted. I wasn't kidding about the red rage—I've been angry before, but *never* like this. The next thing I knew was another new sound: my French horn case slamming into Ryan's wrist, and, I was pretty sure, the snap of a bone.

My stomach lurched and I swallowed hard. Everything seemed hyper-bright, hyper-clear. Ryan's voice seemed both loud and far away as he hollered, "Fuck, you bitch! You broke my arm."

Good, I thought.

One of the other kids took off down the hall, clearly not wanting to be a part of this anymore. Unfortunately, a janitor rounded the corner, no doubt coming to see what the commotion was about, and the kid plowed right into him.

It was kind of a blur after that. A school security guard arrived—yes, we have them, sad to say—and the principal, Mr. Blankenship. Because we also have security cameras, and the attack was recorded.

Good, I thought again.

We were all hustled down to Mr. Blankenship's office. Steve went in first, and the rest of us sat in chairs in the outer office, under the watchful eye of Ms. Jiminez, the office admin. She was in her late twenties, and pretty. An alum of the school, if I remembered correctly.

There were two sets of chairs, one on either side of the door, and obviously I sat in one area and the hoodlums sat in the other. They spent their time with their heads huddled together, occasionally glancing at me with dirty looks. No doubt they were synching up their stories.

I wondered if Ryan's arm was really broken. Although it was entirely unlike me, I hoped so.

My rage had faded along with my adrenaline, leaving me shaky and angry, but also relieved this would get dealt with and that Steve was okay.

The AC was turned up too high, adding to my shakiness. The problem with Southern California is it's hard to dress for the weather. Hot and arid outside, chilling inside. I pulled my sleeves down over my hands.

Steve came out of the office, and Mr. Blankenship motioned the boys in. Steve gave them a wide berth, not looking directly at them. The door to the office closed the boys, and Steve reached for the door to the hallway.

"Steve." I held out my hand, and he finally focused on me, blinking as if he'd forgotten I'd been involved in all this.

He was still small for his age, with a smattering of zits and thick, dirty-blond hair that seemed to want to poof rather than anything else. I'm no fashion expert, but a closer cut might have helped? Also, he still had braces.

Three strikes, and all that. Oh, wait, four: he's a band geek.

He's a nice kid, for all he's two years younger than me. Mostly quiet; we hadn't talked about much other than the music I was helping him with. I hadn't twigged that he was gay, but then, I hadn't been thinking about it, and besides, who cared? I mean, I liked girls, and I didn't necessarily hide it, but neither did I shout it from the rooftops.

I have a Facebook page, but only to follow some scientists and stuff. My day-to-day would interest no one...and I don't think anyone's day-to-day is all that real and honest anyway.

Maybe he wasn't gay, but call it a hunch, it really seemed like those guys had called him those slurs for a reason.

"Brittani," he said. His voice was a little weak. "You're okay?"

"I'm fine. You?"

He touched his swelling purpling jaw. "I'll survive." His eyes dropped, then met mine again. "Thanks for trying to help."

"Those guys are assholes," I said. "What they said—"

"Forget it," he said. "Like you said, they're just assholes."

"But—"

"I've got to go," he said, and yanked the door open and hurried out before I could say anything.

Okay. He was upset, didn't want to talk about it where Ms. Jiminez or someone else would hear.

While I waited, I pulled up the student website on my phone and scrolled through pictures until I found the three assholes. Ryan Keller, José Santiago, and Zach Gorman. They weren't listed as participating in any activities. I did notice something I hadn't realized in the heat of the moment: all three had really short hair. Not exactly buzzed, but close.

Bile burned in my throat. I really hoped it was some kind of fashion thing.

I cleared my throat as best I could. "Do you have any water?" I asked Ms. Jiminez.

She reached under the counter separating the outer office from her area, and produced a bottle.

"Thanks," I said. "You're a lifesaver."

"Never expected to see you in here," she said.

I shrugged. "Witness to a crime," I said.

She went back to whatever she was doing. It occurred to me that she probably knew more about what went on in this school than anybody. I made a mental note to bring her cookies soon—I love to bake, and being on her good side could prove useful down the line.

The principal's office door opened again, and out came the homophobic assholes.

Zach flashed me the bird, his hand hidden from Mr. Blankenship and Ms. Jiminez's view. José snickered, but Ryan just shot daggers at me with his gaze as he passed. I met his eyes as I stood, showing no fear, using my height to my advantage. I'd have to watch out for him.

Mr. Blankenship waved me into his office ahead of him. He was short, compact, with salt-and-pepper hair that was easing back at the temples and dark eyebrows that hadn't caught up with the greying notice yet. I think my being taller than him made him nervous, because he hurried around his desk and motioned to the chair I should sit in.

I'd been in the main office before, but never in here. His desk and bookcases were pale wood. An etched nametag facing me said "Robert Blankenship." On the windowsill was a cactus producing yellow flowers. There was a lingering smell of curry; probably his lunch. In the silence, his computer fan seemed loud.

He folded his hands on his desk. "Ms. Menchin. I'm disappointed in you."

Well, that wasn't what I'd been expecting. I mean, I hadn't assumed he was going to give me a medal for doing what I'd like to think most people would. But I thought I was here to give my account of what had happened so the assholes got their due.

"I'm afraid you're suspended for five days, effective immediately."

"*What?* What for?"

He looked at me as if I'd just asked him why water was wet. "For fighting."

"What? I wasn't fighting!"

"Mr. Keller said you hit him with your tuba case."

It took everything in my power not to roll my eyes. "French horn," I said.

I didn't add that if it had been a tuba, Ryan would be hurting a lot worse. I was pretty sure that wouldn't help my case. I was probably already not helping my case.

"French horn case, then," Mr. Blankenship said evenly. "Did you or did you not hit him with it?"

"I was trying to help Steve," I said. "Those three assholes were beating him up."

"Language, Ms. Menchin."

I sucked a deep breath in through my nose. "Sorry. Bullies who ganged up on a smaller kid who had not provoked them in any way."

"I appreciate that neither you nor Mr. Schotz initiated the altercation, but you could have found a security guard to help."

I bit my tongue, feeling hot all over. "I didn't think there would be time before Steve got seriously hurt."

"Be that as it may," Mr. Blankenship said—(a phrase I hate)—"as you no doubt know, we have a zero tolerance policy here. All parties are receiving the same penalty."

I was vibrating in my chair. Was he *kidding*?

"Even though this was a hate crime?" I asked.

He reared back, clearly shocked. "Hate crime?" he said.

"They called Steve..." I remembered not to use "language." "Homophobic slurs."

He blinked. "Mr. Schotz didn't say anything about that."

Now it was my turn to blink. "Oh. Well, maybe he's so shaken up, he forgot."

It was possible, of course, that Steve wasn't gay, so the f-word didn't register with the same hideous ferocity. But even if he wasn't, those assholes had used hate language.

"I'll confirm with him when I call his parents," Mr. Blankenship said. He sighed, and his shoulders dropped a little. "You're a model student here, Ms. Menchin, and I'm sorry, but my hands are tied: the rules are the rules. I'll make sure your teachers work with you to make sure you complete any homework assignments due during your absence."

Yeah, but I'd also miss band practice, and the rules were stupid, and...

I kept my mouth shut. It wasn't easy, but *I'm* not stupid. No sense making this worse for myself.

The head of the school wasn't in my corner. I'd have to fix this on my own.

Apparently I have this Fixer reputation to live up to.

The hallways were mostly empty, weak spring sunlight barely slanting in the doors at the end. The buzzing fluorescent lights inset in the ceiling did their best to compensate. There might still be basketball practice going on, but it was late enough that all the after-school clubs had ended.

My locker was in another wing, but the sophomore lockers were here, and down a ways I saw Steve. He was kind of just standing in front of his open locker, frozen.

I headed toward him. "Hey, Steve!"

He jumped and whirled. His eyes were wide and he looked as

though he was about to bolt. Crap. Of course he'd be on edge. What had I been thinking?

"It's just me," I said, unnecessarily because he could *see* that. But I felt as if I had to say *something*. I walked up to him, my French horn case bumping against the outside of my knee.

"Do you need a ride home?" I asked.

He looked less wild-eyed. "No, thanks. My dad's coming to pick me up."

"I hope he's not mad at you," I said.

"He's glad I'm okay," Steve said, and my heart grew several sizes bigger because of Mr. Schotz.

I wasn't going to ask Steve if he was gay, because that was none of my goddamned business, but I had to know—

"So, why didn't you tell Mr. Blankenship what those assholes called you?"

Steve paused in the act of pulling a heavy blue science book from his locker. He closed his eyes for a moment. "I didn't hear them call me anything."

"Of course you did. They said f—the F-word."

"I didn't hear it." He shoved the book in his bag, still not looking at me.

"But if it was a hate crime, they could be expelled, or—"

He slammed his locker shut and turned to face me. "Brittani. Look. I really appreciate you helping me, and I'm really sorry you got suspended too. But let it go, okay? It's over."

And with that, he slung his orange backpack over one shoulder and headed to the double glass doors leading outside, leaving me with my mouth hanging open.

It wasn't my best look.

Thank goodness no one was around to witness it.

ZERO TOLERANCE

I drove home in my parents' second car that was mostly mine, a teal Nissan Sentra that was safe and got good gas mileage. I appreciated the freedom I got from it.

We lived in a boring neighborhood of two-story Mediterranean-style houses, the kind you find all over Southern California. The front was landscaped with rocks and native plants; the backyard was prickly grass that stayed mostly green because of a watering system.

I dropped my French horn case and book bag in the tiled foyer by the stairs and headed for the kitchen. It was nice and big for baking, with black granite countertops and warm reddish cabinets, and pendant lights over the island that made it easy to read recipes.

I grabbed a can from the pantry, popped the top, and dug in with a spoon from the drying rack by the sink. Then I proceeded to stress-eat cold Chef Boyardee ravioli straight from the can while pacing the kitchen.

There's nothing like it. Don't judge me.

Both of my parents were out of town for work. That's right, they left their teenage daughter alone for two weeks, with no fear of wild parties or any sort of shenanigans—except maybe the bad eating. They'd left frozen meals for me.

Right now, though, I needed the Chef.

If my parents had been home, they might have gone to bat for me against the school, protesting the suspension, so I was almost glad they weren't. Zero tolerance policies were bullshit, yes, but right now changing school—or possibly district—policy wasn't my goal. (I made a mental note to save it for later.)

Not having to go to school tomorrow or four days next week was something of a boon, really. I could get my homework done and turned in. I could practice my French horn. Not having to sit through classes meant I had free time to do something else.

Figure out if those assholes were as assholery as I feared, and if they were, figure out how to Take. Them. Down.

For all I fix things, I'm pretty Lawful Good, if you know what I mean. Okay, Chaotic Good. I don't help people who've done illegal things, and I don't do illegal things to help them.

(Okay, there was some blackmail, but it was only to stop a girl's parents from being all high-and-mighty against her lesbian relationship. It's not like I asked for *money*.)

This time, though, I was facing going against my moral core.

It pissed me off.

I was up most of the night, and it took baking a batch of chocolate-maple fudge, a lemon-blueberry cheesecake, and a double batch of peanut butter cookies before I was tired enough to shut up my brain and fall over.

I woke up just as determined, however.

Research first. If at any point it looked as though they were your basic garden variety asshole bullies, I'd stop.

Otherwise, rules would be bent as far as they needed to go.

Our house was ridiculously big for three people, which meant I had a second room attached to my bedroom, which I use as a study. Which was useful, because I was a computer nerd along with being a math nerd and music nerd. The bare spots on the walls not covered by shelves have posters of people I admire, like engineers and scientists. And Tony Stark.

Can of ravioli in hand, I went up to my study and dove in.

First I checked out all the social media belonging to the assholes. Their Facebook pages were bland, which could mean they were smart enough to not post some things publicly.

They were *not* smart enough to avoid taking those stupid quizzes, like What's Your Porn Name. You know, the ones that combine the name of your first pet with the first street you lived on and your mother's maiden name.

You know, all of those answers that are also answers to your security questions if you've forgotten your password....

Their Facebook pages had some icky stuff, mostly anti-feminist, pro-kick-out-immigrants memes. Some trolling and harassment of other people, but nothing truly heinous.

No, they saved the heinous stuff for Snapchat.

It took me a while to figure out their user names. I made a fake Snapchat profile in order to follow them, pretending to be an asshole. It left a bad taste in my mouth, and I paused to eat some fudge.

They all let me follow them.

And it was awful.

Memes. Videos of them making fun of anyone not a heterosexual, with every hideous slur you can think of. Sketches of swastikas by Zach labeled "tattoo ideas." Things flashed by, up and gone.

I had to admit, I was surprised José was a part of it, but maybe he'd proven to them that his parents or grandparents or whoever had come here legally. Most of their stuff was anti-Muslim (or anti-anyone-who-wasn't-Christian) anyway.

My stomach churned. I regretted the fudge.

A moment later, I was in the bathroom and the fudge and I were parting ways.

Then I went back and started saving screen shots of everything I could find.

My friend Char came over on Saturday. We had been friends in grade school, but when she got pretty in junior high, she slid over to the popular crowd and I found my way firmly into the nerdy crowd. We reconnected earlier this year when I helped her get out of playing a stupid game involving naked bits and photos.

Which means I'm now popular-adjacent. Yippie.

But I was glad to have Char back in my life.

She took one look at what I'd been eating, sat me down at the kitchen island, and made me eat a turkey sandwich piled high with tomatoes and spinach. While I did, she told me the rumors that were swirling about what had happened.

I swore her to secrecy—I truly believed I could trust her—and told her the whole truth. The whole, unvarnished truth.

She was pale-complexioned, but I swore she got paler.

She hugged me, hard.

Then I sent her home with the cheesecake. I had work to do.

Our school didn't have an AV club per se, but there were the kids who did tech for theater productions, and helped with IT, like streaming the morning announcements.

As a computer nerd, I was nominally a part of that group. But today, my first day back at school, I couldn't be seen anywhere near the equipment.

But I have friends.

I warned them they could get into trouble, and they swore they'd hide their tracks.

So I went to homeroom, the red rage at a low simmer, and waited.

Junior Class President Alexis Sandoval was on tap to read the morning announcements today. We watched on the monitor at the front of the classroom as she began.

And then something happened. Alexis went away, and a video started playing.

A video exposing Ryan Keller, José Santiago, and Zach Gorman as the neo-Nazis they were.

I'd kept Steve's name out of everything. Truly, in the end I didn't think it would matter, because there would be so much focus on the other three that even though they'd jumped him, it was clear they were looking to go after anyone. It could have been because he was gay (or he wasn't and they thought he was), or Jewish (a guess on my part), or because he was still scrawny and nebbish and he made an easy target.

I was on my way to my fifth-period class when Mr. Blankenship stopped me.

"I don't have any proof," he said, "but I'm guessing you were behind this morning's little stunt?"

"If I was, can we just say I've already served my time?"

He closed his eyes, shook his head. "Just go to class, Brittani."

"What's going to happen to the assholes?" I asked.

He didn't chide me on my language this time. "They're facing expulsion," he said. "It takes a little while for the paperwork to get processed."

I smiled and fished a plastic container out of my book bag.

"Cookie?" I offered.

LOST AND FOUND

LAURA WARE

And here's our sweet story, filled with passion.

When I first read Laura Ware's "Lost and Found," I wondered if Laura could pull this off. It's a delicate story that could fall into the "too cute" category.

It never does.

Laura Ware writes successful nonfiction and fiction. Her column, "Laura's Look," appears weekly in the Highlands News-Sun. *Her essay, "Touched by an Angel," appeared in* Chicken Soup for the Soul: Random Acts of Kindness. *Her fiction often contains a touch (or a lot) of mystery, including her novel*, Dead Hypocrites. *Her short fiction has appeared in a variety of venues, including nine previous volumes of* Fiction River. *To find out more about her work, go to laurahware.com.*

When I hear Josh Turner's "Would You Go With Me" on the car radio, I almost make a U-turn and headed back home. Sarah had loved that song, and the man's deep voice is a knife to my heart.

But there would be memories of Sarah at the apartment, too. Her rose-colored wingback chair she liked to curl up in while reading off her Kindle; her favorite coffee mug, which had cartoon pictures of people destroying their computers; the "Happy Hugger" bear I got her at the state fair a couple of years ago.

My counselor told me there would be days like this, when the pain was almost unbearable. But they still come as nasty surprises. After six long months, the pain is as fresh as the day Sarah closed her eyes for the last time and slipped away while I held her hand.

I go on to the office because I'm not sure I can face the apartment in my current mood. I know if I went back I would be paralyzed—part of me wanting to box up everything that was Sarah's and driving down to Goodwill with it, the other part desperately wanting to hang on to anything that she'd touched.

Yeah, I'm a mess. There's a reason I'm seeing a counselor once a week.

I get to my office, located in a strip mall between a local deli and a computer repair shop. Jan, my girl Friday appears to have beaten me in, her silver Honda Accord parked in its usual spot. I park next to her, grab my brown leather laptop bag and prepare to face the day.

I yank open the glass door with my name on it—"Steven Proctor, P.I."—and step inside. It's a little warm in the front of the office, warmer than the current temperature outside. That'll change pretty soon—Central Florida has gentle winters but miserable summers, and the weatherman predicted we'd hit 85 by noon this June day.

Jan turns away from her flat screen monitor with a smile that vanishes the minute she sees my face. "You okay?"

I swallow back a snappy response. "Just one of those days," I tell her. "Anything urgent?"

She shakes her head and gives me a handful of pink message slips. "No. It can all wait. I have things covered here."

"Good." I step around her secondhand metal desk and open the door to my private office. "Don't bother me unless you have to, okay?"

I shut the door on her affirmative response and try not to look at my desk, a mahogany monstrosity Sarah and I refinished one weekend. Plopping into my padded office chair, my gaze is drawn to a picture of Sarah that's parked on the desk.

It was taken before the diagnosis, before we went to the doctor to find out why she couldn't get pregnant. She still has her thick black hair which is looking a little windblown. Her head is tilted back and she's laughing, her brown eyes sparkling with joy and life.

I close my eyes and swallow my tears. Then I reach over and put the picture face down on the desk. I can't look at it today.

Jan taps on my door about 45 minutes later. Without waiting for me to yell come in, she enters. "There's a Miss Bridget Marcum here with her mother Andrea. She needs to see you."

I glance up from my laptop, set on the middle of my blotter. "Jan, tell them I'm busy."

She comes around the desk and checks out my laptop's screen. "The black eight goes on the red nine."

I duck my head. Jan's not old enough to be my mother, but she has a way about her that reminds me of Mom. "Look, this isn't a good day..."

"Steve, you need to see her," Jan says. "It's an important case." Her gaze goes to Sarah's picture, still face down on my desk. "Trust me on this one, okay?"

I grimace. "Jan..."

"Have I ever steered you wrong before?" she asks me, reaching over to shut my laptop. "Please, Steve. You won't be sorry."

I sigh. "You're not going to let me say 'no,' are you?"

"Nope," she grins. I watch her leave my office and say to someone that they can go on in.

The minute Bridget and her mother walk into my office, I want to yell for Jan to come back so I can fire her. I can't believe she sent them in.

Andrea Marcum has thin blond hair and the look of someone who has the weight of the world on her shoulders. She's holding Bridget's hand and giving me a wary look, like she's ready for me to hurt her or her child.

Bridget herself looks to be eight or nine. She's thin and pale, and wearing a blue *Frozen* T-shirt and worn blue jeans. A blue and white headscarf is wrapped around her head.

I had been married to a cancer patient undergoing chemo. I can spot people like her a mile off. I open my mouth to tell the mom that Jan made a mistake—then Bridget steps forward, her blue eyes intense.

"You're Mister Proctor," she says, her voice clear as a bell. "I saw your picture on your website. You have a nice smile."

"Uh," I say, taken aback. The picture had been Sarah's idea, thinking it gave a personal touch to the website. Jan agreed. I joked my ugly face would drive people away, but it apparently hadn't done so in this case.

"I want to hire you," Bridget says. "Your website says you can find things."

"Um," I stammer, looking to her mother. The mom must see something in my expression because she frowns. "Sweetie, maybe we should come back another time..."

"But I haven't told him what got lost," Bridget says. "He can't find it if I don't tell him."

I glance at the closed door, condemning Jan to all kinds of evil fates while I try to figure out how not to hurt this poor kid who has enough pain to deal with. "Look, miss, I can't promise I can find anything you lost. I mean, I'm not going to search your room and house..."

"I didn't lose him there," Bridget says patiently. "It was at the center."

I glance at Bridget's mom. "The Lyons Cancer Treatment Center," she supplies. "Bridget gets her chemotherapy there."

Bridget nods. "I lost my teddy bear there. I want you to find him."

"I...see," I say. For the first time I notice that Bridget is trembling slightly. Cursing myself for being an insensitive jerk, I say, "Why don't you have a seat?"

Bridget immediately plants herself in one of the padded wooden chairs in front of my desk with a relieved sound. Her mom takes the other chair, but leans forward, like she's ready to leap across my desk and rip out my throat if I hurt her kid.

I fold my hands on top of my laptop. I don't take notes, because I don't plan on taking this case. I'll be polite, sure, but I'm not going near this kid. "So tell me about your bear."

Bridget pulls a folded piece of paper from her pocket. "My daddy gave him to me before he went to Af...Af..."

"Afghanistan," her mother says. She's watching me, her hands clasped on her knees. "My husband was deployed over a month ago."

Bridget nods. "Daddy said the bear would keep me company

while I got my medicine." She holds out the folded piece of paper and I take it.

Unfolding it, I see it's a picture printed off a computer. It shows Bridget, without her headscarf, curled up on a blue recliner. The bear she's holding is a decent size, and dressed in green camouflage, which contrasts with its dark brown fur.

"That's my teddy," Bridget tells me. "His name is Rob."

"Rob," I echo. "Um, when is the last time you saw Rob?"

Bridget appears to think over the question. "I think it was the day before yesterday, right Mommy? Mommy had to carry me to the car because I got sleepy after I got my medicine."

"Yes," Bridget's mom agrees. "The bear was with her in the center, but when we got home it was gone." She drops her gaze. "I think he fell out of her bag and I didn't notice."

"It's okay, Mommy," Bridget says. She gets up and goes to pat her mother's hand. "It was an accident."

Her mom shakes her head slightly and I know she's not feeling the weight of the world, she's feeling guilt—and that's far heavier.

I look at the picture. Blast it, I don't want to do this. But the kid is a charmer. I clear my throat. "Bridget, I don't know if I can help you."

She turns to me, her eyes wide. "But I need you to find Rob."

"I know," I say. "It's just that…I normally don't look for teddy bears. Surely the center could help you, or you could get another bear…"

Her face crumples, but her voice is still clear. "I don't want another bear. I want Rob."

"I get that," I say. I'm searching for words. I can't tell her that my wife died of cancer and the last thing I need is a reminder of the fact.

"I brought you money," Bridget says, pulling a rumpled bill from her pocket. "A lady at church gave it to me, she said I could buy something I wanted. I want Rob."

She reaches over and drops the bill on top of my laptop. It's a five. Five lousy dollars. I know without another word it's the only pay I'd get for the case. And it won't even cover my gas.

The mom stares at me. She apparently doesn't like what she sees. "Sweetheart, I think we've taken enough of Mr. Proctor's time. Let's go."

"But Mommy..."

"He's not going to help, hon," she says as she stands. The look she gives me as she says that...well, if looks could kill, I'd be needing CPR.

"Yes, he will," Bridget protests. She turns to me, her lip quivering. "It's enough, right? You can help me?"

The quivering lip does me in. I can hear Sarah's voice in the back of my head. *Are you really going to tell that poor thing no?*

I force a smile on my face. "You're in luck, kid," I say, plucking the bill off my laptop. "Five bucks is the going rate for finding lost teddy bears."

Jan doesn't wait long after a hopeful Bridget leaves with her mom. She stands in front of my desk, searching my face. "Am I fired?"

She's a smart one. "I haven't decided," I tell her. "I took the case —I hope you're satisfied."

"I'm glad, I won't lie," she says. "I think you're doing the right thing—and it will maybe help you too."

I scowl at her. "I don't need any more help. I'm seeing a counselor, I'm doing as well as can be expected."

"Have you been to the cemetery yet?"

The question takes my breath away. My scowl ramps up into a glare. "That's none of your business."

"Steve." She sits down across from me. "I'm trying to help. I know it's hard –"

"You have no clue," I snap.

She flinches as if my tone physically struck her. "You're right. I don't know exactly what you're going through. I've watched you and tried to be there for you. Sarah wouldn't want you to be in pain like this."

I close my eyes. She's right—Sarah wouldn't be happy with me right now. But she isn't here to whip me back into shape. And Jan, for all her good intentions, isn't qualified.

I open my eyes. "Look, you get a pass this time because I know you meant well. But don't ever try to spring something like this on me again. I'm doing the best I can."

She shoots me a doubtful look but says, "All right. Are we good?"

"Yeah," I say. "Go ahead and get me the address of The Lyons Cancer Treatment Center. I need to check it out."

Jan stands and heads for the door. "You want a phone number too?"

"Nope," I tell her. "I'm a lot harder to stonewall in person."

She hesitates in the doorway. "You think they won't help?"

I glance over to where Sarah's picture rests face down still. With a sigh I set it back in place. "Medical people can be very unhelpful. Especially when you want information about their patients."

Jan considers that piece of information. "You think someone took the bear? But why?"

I shrug and hold up the five dollar bill. "That's what I'm getting paid to find out."

The Lyons Cancer Treatment Center is located behind the county hospital. It's an older brick building that has been around since the hospital first opened. As I park in the large parking lot that serves both the center and the hospital I see the larger half-completed building a couple of lots down. A huge sign says it's going to be the new home of the treatment center in the winter of the following year. Getting out of my car, I can hear the whine of an electric saw and figure someone's hard at work over there.

Inside the center, I find myself in a large waiting room filled with dark wooden chairs. There is a brightly colored box in one corner of the room that's overloaded with toys and a painted yellow giraffe on the wall over there adds a small bit of cheer.

It's hard to be here. Sarah got her chemo at her oncologist's office, a place very different from here. But the smells are the same—disinfectant and medicine and that one smell you can't quite describe but screams sickness.

I go to the frosted window ahead and to the left of the door and knock. After identifying myself and making it clear I wasn't leaving without talking to someone, the gray haired dragon who's manning the window tells me to take a seat and wait.

I fiddle with my phone so I don't have to look at anyone else. I don't want to see the hopeful faces, those who are getting better or just starting treatment, or the resigned faces, who are struggling. I saw plenty of both when I took Sarah for her treatments.

Murmured conversations are a soothing drone in the half-filled room, the occasional whimper of a child breaking through it now and then. The door leading outside opens and I catch a whiff of coffee that overpowers the other smells for a minute.

Fifteen minutes after I sit down I hear some guy say, "Mr. Proctor?" I look up and see a man who's maybe in his fifties standing in a doorway to the right of the frosted windows. He's wearing a short-sleeved green dress shirt and navy slacks with a matching tie.

I stand up and approach the man. "You are...?"

"Mark Grayson. I'm the administrator of this facility." He shakes my hand quickly and leads me into a mess of hallways. Several turns later I find myself in a small but nice office, with a mahogany desk and leather chair for Grayson, a padded wooden chair that's a lot more comfortable than the ones in my office for me.

Grayson takes his seat and steeples his fingers. "My receptionist says you're a private investigator and that you insisted on seeing someone in charge."

"Yup," I say. "I need to talk to you about something that happened here."

A line appears between Grayson's hazel eyes. "What would that be?"

"A little girl's teddy bear went missing. Her name is Bridget Marcum. Ring a bell?"

A sigh. "Mr. Proctor, I cannot acknowledge if someone is a patient here. Privacy laws. I'm sure you understand the importance of confidentiality."

I pull a form from my jacket pocket. Like a Boy Scout, I am prepared. "That's why I had Ms. Marcum fill out this release. It authorizes you all to talk to me about Bridget."

Grayson frowns but takes the form. After scanning it, he lays it on his immaculate desk. "Very well. I am aware that Bridget misplaced her toy. We looked for it. It isn't here."

"Her mom wanted to put a poster in the waiting room asking if someone had seen it, but your staff put the kibosh on that. How come?"

The administrator makes an impatient sound. "Children lose things all the time. We can't have our walls cluttered with lost and found posters. We did what we could, but we didn't find the bear. I'm sorry."

"Maybe someone took it," I say. "From what I figure, she had the bear during her treatment but it wasn't in the car when they got home. They went straight home—I asked."

"You think someone stole the child's bear?" Grayson looks pained at the thought. "If that is true, I'm afraid there's no way to determine that."

"Well, there might be," I say. "I noticed you have security cameras outside."

Grayson's face becomes an impassive mask. "And?"

"If I could see your data from that day, maybe something will show up."

Grayson lowers his hands flat on the desk. "Impossible."

"Come on," I say. "It's outside. I could be sitting in my car and see what the camera saw. You saying privacy laws cover that?"

"Mr. Proctor," Grayson says, "I will not compromise the security of this facility so you can go on a fishing expedition. The answer is no."

I grit my teeth. I can play dirty if he insists. "This is a little girl with cancer. That bear was given to her by her dad, who is currently overseas in Afghanistan. You telling me you can't help a soldier's sick daughter out? What kind of patriot are you?"

Grayson's face flushes. "I will not be spoken to in this manner. I care deeply about the patients here—more than you do, I assure you. You have no idea what they go through, what their families go through. To invade their privacy as you suggest –"

"My wife was a cancer patient," I growl. "I *do* have an idea, whether you like it or not." I stand up. "I guess I'll just suggest that the Marcums contact the press. They'll eat this story up—it's got lots of feels to it."

Grayson's eyes widen. "Now just a minute. There is no need to make threats."

"This little girl paid me to find her teddy bear," I say. "I aim to use whatever works to make that happen."

Grayson swallows. "Perhaps...perhaps I could review the tapes? I would inform you if I saw anything amiss."

I shake my head. "No offense, but I don't trust you. You're too worried about the reputation of this place."

The administrator looks like he just sucked a lemon, but he gets to his feet. "Follow me."

I let him lead me to what I think is the back of the facility— these hallways are confusing. Grayson raps his knuckles on an unmarked door, and a guy that looks barely old enough to shave sticks his head out. "Yes, sir?"

Grayson hesitates, and for a second I think he's going to have the guy try to escort me off the premises. Instead, he turns to me and says, "What you are going to see is strictly confidential. I want your word that you'll respect that."

"You got it," I agree. The guy, who I notice is dressed in black slacks and a white shirt with a patch that says "Security" on the sleeve looks at us with a puzzled frown.

Grayson doesn't look happy but he turns to the guy and says,

"Mr. Proctor and I need to review some security footage, Charlie. Please assist us."

Charlie shoots me a dark look but lets us into the dark, cramped room. On a long table along one wall are four flatscreen monitors. One shows the waiting area, and the remaining three have different angles on the parking lot outside.

Sitting in a metal folding chair in front of a keyboard, Charlie asks, "What are we looking for?" An open bag of Frito's lays next to the mouse and he helps himself to a handful while he waits for our answer.

Grayson looks at me and I supply the date. Charlie frowns. "I'll have to check the archives. The cameras only hold two days of data."

"Is that a problem?" Grayson asks, sounding hopeful.

Charlie shakes his head. "No sir, it's all in the cloud."

In the light of the monitors I see Grayson's face fall. "Very well." He turns to me. "Can we narrow it down? Do you have a timeframe of some kind?"

"Sure do," I say. "According to the mom, they left at around 4:30 PM."

"Okay," Charlie says, typing like crazy on the keyboard. The second monitor from the left goes to static and then shows the waiting room in black and white. The timestamp on the upper right hand corner indicates it's showing the correct date at 4:22:00 PM. "What are we looking for?"

I doubt I'm going to win friends with Grayson naming names, so I settle for, "A woman carrying a bag and a sleeping girl."

Charlie nods and speeds up the video. For a few seconds people speed in and out of the doors to the center, or move around the room in jerky fast motions.

At 4:31:32, Charlie pauses the feed. "That them?" he asks, pointing to a figure frozen in midstep.

I lean forward and squint. The picture is in black and white and not the best quality, but the profile of the woman seems right. At the moment we only see her from the waist up. "Yeah. Can we follow them outside?"

"Easy peasy, man," Charlie says. His fingers dance over the keyboard and after another burst of static we're looking at the parking lot in front of the center.

He sticks to real time now, and I watch Andrea Marcum carry Bridget out. A bag with some kind of pattern on it swings from one arm. A teddy bear wearing camouflage is plopped on top of the bag.

As Bridget's mom steps off the curb, the bag hits a car parked next to her. Rob the bear slides off the top of the bag, landing next to the car. Andrea Marcum keeps walking, not realizing what happened.

A skinny person—I'm not sure at first if it's a man or a woman—runs into the picture. They bend down and pick up the bear and lift their head as if they're going to call out after Bridget's mom.

But it looks like they suddenly stop. First they look down at the bear. Then they glance around them as if to see if someone is watching them. I catch a glimpse of their face as they turn toward the camera. "Freeze it," I snap.

Charlie does. I'm looking at the face of a teenage boy, his dark hair down to his T-shirt. He's carrying a small backpack. Grayson makes a sound next to me I can't interpret, but I'm sure it's not good.

After glancing around, the teen stuffs the bear inside the backpack. He then leaves the picture frame.

Grayson looks like he might throw up. Charlie's eyes are wide. "Mr. Grayson! Did you see that?"

Swallowing, Grayson says, "I want a password placed on this portion of the video. No one gets to see it without my permission. Is that clear?"

"Sir," Charlie says, "I'll have to do the whole file—the whole two days' worth."

"Do what you have to," he snaps. Jerking his head toward the door, he leads me outside into the hallway. "Mr. Proctor, you gave me your word you would respect the confidentiality of what you saw. I want you to remember that."

"I'm not shouting it from the housetops," I say, "but I need to know who that kid is."

"I am not sure," Grayson says, pinching the bridge of his nose. "Unfortunately I do not know everyone that comes here."

"And if you did know you wouldn't tell me, would you?"

"Mr. Proctor, I've done all I can," Grayson sounds tired. "Please do not ask my staff to identify the individual. I will alert them to watch for the bear, in case it shows up somehow."

"Can you at least tell me how often someone gets chemo here?" I ask.

"It varies," he says. "I'll show you out."

I don't move. "I need your help in this."

"I can't do anything else," he tells me. "I've already broken protocol letting you see the video—what more do you want?"

"Let me know if the kid comes back here," I say.

Grayson stiffens. "Privacy laws..."

"He's not a patient," I point out. "At least, he didn't look like one."

"Even so, I must respect the privacy of whoever he was with," Grayson insists. "I'm sorry, Mr. Proctor. But I have more to take care of than one child. Can't you understand that?"

"I could still alert the media," I say.

"You gave your word."

"And I will keep it. But I can let slip that you know who the guilty party is and you're protecting him. How will that look to the hospital board?"

Grayson clenches his fists. "You are not a nice man, Mr. Proctor."

"No one is paying me to be nice," I say. "So, what'll it be?"

Grayson stalks down the hallway without a word. I follow—I really want to get out of here, truth be told. Grayson is too worried about the center's reputation to be much help, and I have to figure out my options.

While I really mean that I would go to the press, I'm not sure I could sell Bridget and her mom on it. Plus, part of me recoils at putting the poor kid in the limelight like that. Even for a good cause, it seems wrong.

Next thing I know Grayson is pointing to what looks like a staff entrance. "Please leave."

I raise an eyebrow. "I really hope you reconsider. A little girl's happiness depends on it."

Grayson's finger starts to shake. "I said you should leave."

I figure he's as close to losing it as a guy like him can be. I shrug and pull out one of my cards, holding it out for him to take. "In case you change your mind."

He snatches the card out of my hand. Figuring that's all I can do, I push the door open. Florida sunshine bathes me in a rush of warmth, welcome after the air conditioning I've been in.

I head for my car, my thoughts racing. I can't stake out the place all day—I have other clients. I need to find out more.

I decide I need to consult with my client.

I pull up to the neat cinderblock house about fifteen minutes from my office. It's pale green with dark green shutters. The yard is small but someone recently mowed it.

I called ahead to make sure they'd be home. I barely take my finger off the doorbell when the dark green door flies open to reveal Bridget. "Did you find Rob?"

She's not wearing her headscarf and her bald scalp reminds me of Sarah like a punch to the gut. For a moment, I can't speak.

Bridget frowns up at me. "Are you okay?"

"Yeah," I grind out. "Sorry. Where's your mom?"

"In the kitchen," she says. "Would you like some lemonade? Maybe it will help you feel better."

"Sure," I say, not really caring if I get something to drink or not. Bridget leads me down a short hallway to a small kitchen on the right side. Her mom is there, loading a dishwasher. When she sees us, she grabs a small checked towel from the counter and wipes her hands. "Mr. Proctor. You said you had an update?"

"Yes, ma'am," I say. "Is there someplace we can talk?"

"Of course," Ms. Marcum says. "Would you like something to drink?"

"He wants lemonade," Bridget says.

Her mom looks at me. "That'll be fine," I say.

"Bridget, take Mr. Proctor to the family room. I'll be right there."

"Okay Mommy," Bridget says. She leads me to what I guess is the family room. A brown recliner sits near a matching couch, a small round table between them. The television at one end of the room is set to what looks like the Disney Channel. Several dolls lay scattered on the floor in various stages of dress.

I settle into the recliner while Bridget turns off the television. A moment later, her mother comes in with a wooden tray that holds three glasses of lemonade and a plate of chocolate chip cookies. She sets the tray on a coffee table in front of the couch and hands me a glass while offering the plate of cookies.

I haven't had lunch yet and the cookies look homemade. I grab one and bite it in half. Perfect.

Bridget is watching me from the couch. "Do you like the cookies? I helped make them."

I swallow, wondering if I'd be a pig to grab two more off the plate. "They're delicious."

She smiles, and I notice her mom looks a little less stressed with that. She sits next to her daughter, an arm around her shoulders. "Did you find out anything?"

I stall by taking a sip of lemonade. "Someone picked up Rob. But I don't know who they are."

"Someone took him?" Bridget asks, her smile gone in an instant. Her mother squeezes her shoulders.

"It looks that way," I say. "They were carrying a backpack. They put Rob into it. Do you know anyone who had a backpack that day?"

Bridget frowns. "Was it a grownup? Or a kid like me?"

"Not a grownup," I tell her.

"Didn't the staff know?" her mom asks. "Didn't you ask them?"

"The administrator wouldn't let me. Privacy concerns," I say.

Bridget's mother snorts. "'Privacy concerns.' I think they're afraid of getting sued. If I had the money..."

"Can you find them?" Bridget asks me.

"If you help me, sweetheart. Who might have a backpack that day?"

Her face screws up in thought. "Will brings a backpack. It's not a big one though."

I nod. "Do you remember who was with Will that day?"

She shakes her head. "I can ask him about it though, when I see him again. We have the same doctor."

I'm not sure that's a good idea. I look at her mom. "If you like, we could go to the press with this—they'd love the story. It might flush out the thief."

"No!"

I look at Bridget. She's glaring at me, her fists clenched. "I don't want to be a cancer kid on TV or in the paper. Everyone looks at you like you're a freak."

"Honey, it's okay, we don't have to do that," her mom says, rubbing her back. "I'm sure Mr. Proctor can find Rob another way."

"Can you?" Bridget asks. "Can you find Rob?"

I look into those blue eyes. "Bridget, I'll do my best. Your mom's right. You don't have to go to the press if you don't want to."

I mean it, too. I'll do my best.

But I'm not sure how I'm going to solve this one.

Two days later, I'm having a better day. Not a great one, by any stretch of the imagination. But at least I don't want to crawl into a hole and pull the hole in after me.

I'm doing paperwork on a case I've just wrapped up when Jan taps on my door. "A Mr. Grayson on line one," she says. "He says it's urgent."

I grab the receiver. "Proctor."

Grayson is talking very low, very fast. "The young man you are interested in is here. I'm not sure for how long—Security just let me know."

"I'm on my way," I say, standing and checking to make sure my keys are in my pocket. "Can you stall him?"

A brief silence. "Mr. Proctor, please do not cause a scene at the center."

"I won't," I promise. "Just give me ten minutes."

"I will do what I can," he sighs.

I hang up and go dashing out, shouting over my shoulder to Jan that I'd be back later. By speeding through a couple of yellow stoplights and breaking a traffic rule or two, I get to the center in about seven minutes. Parking where I can see the door, I wait.

I don't wait long. Five minutes haven't passed before the kid I saw on the video comes out. He doesn't have the backpack, and there is no sign of the bear. He's walking along like he doesn't have a care in the world.

I get out of my car and head in his direction. "Excuse me."

He pauses, looking at me with a questioning glance. Seeing him in real life I notice the poor kid's got a bad case of acne on his cheeks.

I get within a few feet of him and stop. I decide there's no time to be coy. "Where's the bear?"

He blinks at me, his body tensing. "What bear?"

"The one you found, kid. The one you didn't give back to the little girl."

He shifts his weight from foot to foot. "I dunno what you're talking about, man."

"Yeah you do," I say. "That little girl's daddy got her that bear, did you know that?"

"Well..." the boy looks over my shoulder. "Maybe he could get her another one?"

I'm afraid to get closer—he might try to run. "He's in Afghanistan."

The kid's shoulders sag. "At least she has a dad," he mutters.

I cock my head. "Why'd you take it?"

"What's it to you?" the kid snaps. "I don't even know who you are."

"My name's Steve. I'm a private investigator," I say. "What's your name?"

He licks his lips. "Kevin. And I—I don't have to talk to you, do I?"

"Sure, if you're okay with breaking a little girl's heart," I say. "A sick little girl—but you know about someone being sick, don't you Kevin? Will, is he your brother?"

"Leave him outta this," Kevin says. "I told him she didn't want it anymore. He didn't have nothing to do with it."

I raise my hands. "Look, I need some answers. And I need the bear. I'm sorry about your brother —"

"You don't know," he says. "You don't know how it is when they're sick, and they just want a bear to keep them company during the night. But we don't have the money for stuff like that."

I thought of Sarah, when there were bad days. Days when I'd have done anything to take the pain away, to win a smile from her. "So you stole the bear."

"She dropped it," he counters. "I found it. That's not stealing, is it?"

"It didn't belong to you, did it?" I ask, my tone gentle. "And you knew it was Bridget's but you didn't give it back."

He blinks his eyes hard. "Will needs it. He needs the bear at night."

"What if we got him another bear?" I ask.

"But this bear is special," Kevin says. "I had a cool story how he came to fight the bad dreams. Will's five, he believes it. I can't take the bear away from him."

I think about it. I have an idea, but it's going to be tough. "I think I can replace it with another special bear. Will you let me try?"

Kevin sticks his hands in his pockets. "Are you gonna call the cops on me?"

I shake my head. "I just want the bear back. If I can help your brother, and get the bear back, then everyone will be satisfied."

He cocks his head, thinking about it. "Okay. What do you want to do?"

I tell him to meet me with his brother at the nearby McDonald's and to bring Rob with them. I detour to my apartment before meeting them there.

When I slide into the booth at the restaurant, Will is clutching Rob like a lifeline. I notice he's wearing a red and blue baseball cap that's almost too big for him. Next to him, Kevin has a large order of fries.

"Hi Will," I say. "I'm Steve. How are you doing?"

He scowls at me. "Kevin says you wanna take away my bear."

I shoot a dirty look at the teenager, who shrugs and ducks his head. Turning back to Will, I say to him, "Here's the thing. Rob belongs to a little girl who's missing him terribly. He needs to go back and take care of her."

Tears sparkle in Will's eyes. "But I need him. He fights the bad dreams."

"I know," I say. "But that's why I brought a friend of mine to help you out." I reach into the Walmart bag I'd carried in and pulled out Sarah's "Happy Hugger" bear.

There's suddenly a lump in my throat. Sure, I could've gone to the store and bought some bear off the shelf. But Will needs a special bear, not a common one. And I have a story for this one.

"You see," I say, my voice rough, "Happy Hugger belonged to a woman named Sarah. She loved him very much. But then she had to go away and leave him, and he's all alone now."

Will studies Sarah's bear, the tears at bay for the moment. "He's not a soldier bear."

"No," I say. "But he is strong. And he has a lot of love. So much love the bad dreams can't be around him. He just needs someone to give that love to."

Will reaches out a tentative hand to brush Happy Hugger's fur. "Soft," he says. "Did he stop Sarah's bad dreams?"

I remember the nights we'd be in bed together, me hugging her from behind while she clutched that silly bear to her. "I think he did. I helped, but Sarah was bigger than you. I think he can stop your bad dreams."

Will looks from Happy Hugger to Rob. "Kevin said she didn't want him anymore."

Kevin's cheeks redden. "I was wrong, kiddo."

"He was wrong," I tell Will. "She misses him a lot. She paid me to find him and bring him home to her."

"She paid you?" Will asks, his eyes wide.

"Uh-huh," I nod.

Will takes a look at Rob and then squeezes him hard. With a long face he holds him out toward me.

I gently take him while sliding Happy Hugger to Will. It hurts, but at the same time I can see Sarah in my mind's eye smiling and nodding. I know she'd want me to do this.

Will gathers up Happy Hugger and buries his face in the bear's fur. "Thank you," he says, his voice muffled.

"You're welcome," I say. "Thank you for the little girl. You did a brave thing."

Kevin reaches out to rub Will's back. "Thanks, Steve. I think we'll be okay."

I nod and slide out of the booth. I have two stops to make.

Bridget is almost incandescent with joy when she sees her bear. "Thank you, thank you," she keeps saying, throwing her arms around my waist.

I gently untangle her and hand over Rob. Bridget's mom is wiping at a few tears with her fingers. "Thank you Mr. Proctor. I know we owe you for your services..."

"Nope,' I say, watching Bridger dancing in the hallway hugging Rob tightly to her. "Five dollars. Paid in full."

"That's...kind of you," she says. "Would you like something to drink?"

I glance at my watch. "I have to go, I'm afraid. But thanks."

On the way to my next stop I call Jan and let her know what's going on. She tells me to take my time.

There are a couple of people at the cemetery when I get there. I have to go to their office and locate the grave—after six months I don't remember where it is. But the staff is kind and helpful and before I know it I'm standing at Sarah's grave.

I bend down and brush a few stray blades of grass from the flat rose-colored slab. I trace her name with my fingers.

It hurts, but there's something else I'm feeling, too. Like it's right for me to be here. It's a step to healing a wound that's been bleeding for six months. And for the first time since I lost Sarah, I think that healing is possible.

"Hey, hon," I say, my voice rough. "Let me tell you what's been going on..."

TILTING AT WINDMILLS

LAURYN CHRISTOPHER

I couldn't follow Laura Ware's charming story with a story filled with murder and mayhem. I needed a transition story here. "Tilting at Windmills" does not include murder, but there is a lot of mayhem, and two absolutely delightful characters who cause it.

Lauryn Christopher writes a lot of mysteries. Her work has appeared in five previous volumes of Fiction River. *You can find links to more of her work on her website, www.laurynchristopher.com. Her Hit Lady for Hire novel series shares a voice with this story—wry, knowing, and deeply insightful about the human condition.*

It was only a Picasso.

And not even the supposed original—which, when I heard about the rumored Tbilisi discovery several years ago excited me less than it probably should have. But that sketch, which was done in shades of bluish-green, lacked the resonance for me of the stark lines of the two-dollar, black-and-white print that had been tacked to my dorm room wall for most of my college career.

And now it was hanging in my ex-husband's living room. A large, beautifully framed, black-and-white "fuck you" that appeared in too many of our children's weekend-with-daddy selfies to be anything other than deliberate on his part.

My own copy of the print, of course, had not weathered the years well. Torn corners, multiple creases, even a carefully taped four-inch tear had all taken their toll on the 11x17 poster-size version I'd carted around since high school. A poorly-thrown water balloon had puckered the paper, and a toddler with magic markers and a skill for climbing had added pink and green patches to both the landscape and the wall surrounding it before the print was finally taken down from the wall and carefully stored away with other memories, only to be lost in a move sometime between then and the divorce.

But no matter how battered, there was something in the quick, yet deliberate scribbles that shaped Don Quixote on his horse, sturdy Sancho at his side, and the field populated with windmills ready for the tilting that always spoke to me. When reality crowded in too closely, the old knight reminded me to dream. When despair threatened, steadfast Sancho was there to watch over me.

And for every battle I faced, in the shape of windmills on the horizon, the sun always shone above me, lighting the way.

Perhaps it was silly to read so much into a painting—I was, after all, interpreting it to fit my own need, regardless of whatever had been in the mind of the artist when he created it. Had it been nothing more than a quick toss-off to pay the rent? A few bucks earned as the result of a simple telephone call?

Bonjour, Pablo, we are putting together a special issue of the magazine to celebrate Cervantes' work. I know it is an imposition, my friend, but I hoped I could prevail upon you to contribute a piece—a small *piece, of course—that we could use for the cover? It pains me to mention that we are a literary magazine, so cannot pay much, but your name, your art, they might help us sell a few copies...*

Why of course, Louis, we starving artists must help each other because who else will, no? I am in the middle of something else, but wait, let me just sketch something for you quickly while we talk...Ah, here we go. It is not in my usual style, but I think you will like it, and it should reproduce well. I will messenger it over as soon as the ink dries. Give my love to Elsa. We must all have dinner the next time I am in Paris...

Or so the scene played out in my mind, Picasso reaching for pen and ink while discussing art and politics with the poet, Louis Aragon, dashing off the sketch, the quick, bold strokes conveying the artist's confidence onto the page while simultaneously demanding the viewer exercise their own imagination to provide the color.

Was that how it happened? Probably not. For all I know, the two men may not even have known each other personally, but that never really mattered. It was as though the sketch had shared this fanciful story of its creation with me, inviting an intimacy that captured my imagination.

Larry and I had been dating for a few months when I'd told him of the imaginary conversation between Picasso and Aragon, and he'd stared at me like I was a crazy person. I should have recognized then that he didn't have a creative bone in his body and just how poor a match we would be. But, like Quixote, I was lost in the illusion, and could not hear the creaking windmills for what they were.

So now, here we were, ten years, three children, and a divorce later, and he'd gone and picked up an over-the-fireplace-sized copy of my favorite painting—one he knew I no longer had even a print of—just so he could rub it in my nose that the fantasy life I'd dreamed of was nothing more than a tin plate and rickety horse in a field of ragged windmills.

I knew a lot about tilting at windmills.

There were battles I had been willing to pursue with Larry, both during our marriage and afterward; and others where, unlike Quixote, I had seen the wisdom of withdrawing from the field. So when I saw the print hanging prominently in the background of a picture on seven-year-old Sophie's phone, I did my best to ignore it in the moment. (And yes, my children *do* have a cheap, prepaid cell phone that I always make sure Sophie carries when they go to their father's house. There are reasons. Don't judge.)

So I overreacted later. With a couple glasses of wine. One of which came perilously close to becoming a less-than-artistic splatter on the rental-white walls of my weird little rat-maze of an apartment, which was more like a string of rooms on a winding hallway than a planned living space, but it was cheap and I could afford it. I refrained from redecorating with the wine, but only because neither losing my deposit nor cleaning up the mess were at the top of my bucket list.

Instead, I called the one person I knew wouldn't try to talk me off the ledge. Roz would gladly go out there with me, and we'd sit there, Thelma and Louise-style, berating our exes—Andy the Accident who she'd eloped with straight out of high school and divorced a year later, Cheating Chuck, her children's father, and generally speaking, a cheap copy of my Lousy Larry—all while kicking our feet in the breeze. And if the conversation threatened to turn even the slightest bit rational, we would stop it in its tracks and instantly jump off into an even more profound overreaction than I could come up with on my own.

"He bought a Picasso. *My* Picasso," I said as soon as she picked up, trusting that even if she'd not bothered to look at the caller ID, that my wine-soaked voice would identify me.

"My god, Kate! Since when did either of you have the money to own a Picasso?" Roz asked. "And why are you living in that shitty apartment if you've got that kind of cash lying around? For that matter—"

"It's not a *real* Picasso," I said, not waiting for her to stop because I know her well enough to know that she'd just keep going forever if I let her. And right now it was my turn to whine. "It's just my favorite one. And now he's hung this huge print of *my* favorite painting in *his* living room. He never even liked that picture." I paused to gulp down some more wine. Roz started talking again while I refilled my glass.

I missed most of what she was saying, but latched on to her last sentence.

"You never should have married him."

"Ash if I don'no that now," I slurred. "Fat lot of good that does me in retrosight...hindsight. Whatever." I was starting to lose words, which meant the wine was finally kicking in. "He got the picture jus' to piss me off, an' it worked. I'm royally piss-ed. Bes' hunnerd bucks he ever spent."

I was losing my grip on my wineglass along with the thread of the conversation.

"I gotta go," I mumbled. "Gotta sleep. Gotta work tomorrow, an' am gonna have a hell of a headache..."

"Take an aspirin or something," Roz said. "I'll come by after work and we'll figure out a proper retribution for Larry." She probably said more than that, but it was lost on me.

"Retribulation. Shure," I said.

I might have actually agreed to something else before we hung up, but all I wanted at the moment was an Advil and a pillow. Preferably in that order, because I still had enough functional brain cells to know that finding them in the reverse would have been a pain in the ass.

I had never told Roz about my Picasso print. So the next day, after work, while my three kids bonded with her two over macaroni and cheese, and threw dinner rolls at each other across the table, she and I retreated to the living room with our own dinner and a couple cups of coffee. We settled in on my sagging thrift-store sofa, and I gave her the short version of the story.

"So he really did buy that picture just to screw with you," she said. "What a shithead."

You can see why we're friends.

"If I ignore it long enough, he'll eventually get tired of it and—"

"And...nothing," Roz said, cutting me off. "Guys like that get off on pushing buttons; he's pushing yours and he knows it. The only way you'll get him to back off is to take action."

"Sure. Like there's anything I could do to him that wouldn't bounce back and hurt the kids one way or another."

"You were married to him for ten years. What bugs him?"

"Besides living with me? Nothing I could do from a distance. And I'm *not* enlisting the kids, so don't even suggest it. I don't even want them knowing that seeing the picture bothers me."

"You know me better than that." She looked almost insulted, but the glint in her eyes gave her away.

"Yup. Which is why I cut that line off at the knees, before it had an opportunity to develop," I said, raising my mug in salute. I love Roz like a sister, but she doesn't always play fair. I was all for not playing fair, but there were a few lines I wasn't willing to cross.

We tossed random ideas back and forth like ping-pong balls. Planting tiny windmills like flamingoes on Larry's lawn was the best of them, which should give some idea of just how lame the rest were. The problem with pranking him, at least as I saw it, was that all it would accomplish was to prove to him just how successful he had been at upsetting me.

It wasn't like he hadn't done things that had upset me before, and I knew he would again. It just pissed me off that he would use something so special to me as that painting to be so deliberately hurtful.

"I'll just Photoshop the painting out of the background of the kids' pictures," I said finally. "I'm not very good, but I think I can replace it with a blank wall."

Roz choked on her coffee, and as she sat there, holding up her hand and coughing, she was staring at me as if I'd just said something profound.

"What?"

"That's it!" she barked, the words coming out in the last half-cough.

"What? Photoshop? I know—"

"We need to take the painting," she said.

"Take it? What's that got to do with Photoshop?"

"Really take it. Off the wall. Out of his house. Leave him with a blank wall—or better yet, replace it with something he'll hate."

I started to laugh. "One of those velvet paintings, you know, the kind they sell on the side of the road. He hates those. Would always go on and on about how tacky they were."

"They are tacky."

"Of course they are. That's what makes them so perfect for this...." I'd gotten up and was pacing around the room, poking my head in at the dining room just long enough to catch a flying dinner roll and remind the kids that they were supposed to be eating their food and not throwing it.

"I haven't seen any of those in a long time," Roz said.

"Me neither, not on the side of the road, anyway," I said. "But I sometimes see them in the art vendors' stalls at the Farmer's Market. If the weather is good this weekend, want to go with me?"

"Can't. Have to work," she said. "But go—and find the most god-awful one you can. Elvis and Jesus. Or one of those *Mona Lisa*'s that looks like it was painted by a fifth-grader."

"My luck, all I'll find will be still lifes."

"Don't be a Debbie Downer," she said, getting up and heading toward the kitchen. "He needs to be taught a lesson, and the universe is on your side."

I must have given her a "yeah, sure," look, because she stopped in the doorway and turned to face me.

"Is all that bull you keep telling me about 'positive visualization' just crap?"

"Well, there's more to it than...."

"Damn straight there is. You've got to get out there and do something about it. Kick Larry's ass," she said, waving her empty plate around because she was incapable of talking without using her hands. "Just thinking happy thoughts isn't gonna cut it. Let's *do* this. Are you in?"

I hesitated only a moment, then channeled my inner Quixote and took up my metaphorical lance. "I'm in."

Three days later, Roz was waiting outside my office building, motor running, when I ran outside.

"I've got 53 minutes," I said, setting an alarm on my cell phone to alert me when it was quarter to one, so I'd know when we had to wrap up and head back. "Any later, and the Pointy-Haired Boss will get his knickers in a twist about me taking a long lunch and I'll have to stay late tonight, which will put me into overtime with the sitter and—"

"Yeah, yeah, yeah. Don't be a Nervous Nellie," Roz said. She hit the gas and we sped out of the parking lot. As we caromed around curves, she glanced over at me. "You're dressed all wrong for breaking and entering," she said.

I looked down at my black cardigan, business casual black slacks, and sensible black shoes and then over at her. She was wearing tight-fitting black jeans, black sneakers, and a black turtle-neck shirt. I sighed. "You said 'wear black.' I'm wearing black. What's wrong with my clothes?"

"You look like you're ready for a board meeting, not cat burglary. Here, put on some gloves. And cover your hair." She handed me a black knit cap, twin to the one that she'd shoved her masses of thick red hair under. A pair of bright pink rubber kitchen gloves poked out of the hat.

"Because these are totally inconspicuous," I said, dropping the gloves in my lap. Her own gloves were neon yellow.

I pulled on the cap, poking the ends of my brown hair up under the edges. "You're having too much fun exercising your criminal vocabulary," I said. "And we're not breaking and entering. It used to be my house. I have a key."

"He'll have changed the locks."

"Maybe, but he's cheap. He might not have."

"Bet'cha Mommy and Daddy Warbucks made him change them when they fronted the money for their baby boy so he could stay there and not have to move his lazy ass," she said.

I shrugged, hoping she wasn't right, but fearing that she might be. I wasn't entirely sure how I'd ended up agreeing to this caper in the first place, and if there was any possibility that we might end up actually committing a crime...well, I'll admit, I was beginning to get cold feet.

We reached my old neighborhood in seven minutes—record time, since my best door-to-door commute when I'd lived there had been eleven minutes. Roz made a decent wheel-man.

The house, a seventies' split-level in a neighborhood of seventies' split-levels, was looking a little run down. The lawn was running long in some places, had patchy brown spots in others, and the decorative plantings along the sidewalk and in the big raised island in the center of the yard were all dead. The same old, rusted security service sign that had been there when we first bought the place still leaned crookedly against the brick wall a couple of feet from the front door. There were a bunch of cardboard boxes stacked to one side of the carport, next to the garbage cans, but no car, and all the lights were off.

"Doesn't look like he's home," Roz said.

"He shouldn't be," I said. "He almost never comes home in the middle of the day—it's twenty-five minutes each way, in good traffic. A total waste of a lunch break."

We pulled into the carport, just like we owned the place. I hadn't been back since I'd moved out eight months before, back in the days when I did own the place. It felt weird, surreal, more like déjà vu than familiarity, if that makes any sort of sense.

With a deep breath, I pulled on my rubber gloves, got out of the car, and climbed the three steps to the kitchen door.

The key didn't work. And there was no spare in the usual place on the brick ledge above the door.

"Okay, well, that was a fun idea. Where shall we grab lunch?" I said, turning toward Roz.

But she was already rummaging in the trunk of her car, emerging a moment later with a long, thin strip of metal in one hand and a crowbar in the other.

"Plan B," she announced, shoving the trunk closed with an elbow. I stood there on the step, watching in stunned silence as she marched past me and toward the backyard. It was only after she disappeared out of sight around the back of the house that I finally came to my senses and followed.

She was peering into one of the lower-level window wells. "What rooms do these belong to?" she asked, pointing at the window she was looking at and then gesturing to a second window, further on.

"These both open into the family room," I said. "Larry's office, the laundry room, and a bathroom are all on the front side, bedrooms upstairs. What are you thinking?"

"I'm thinking someone needs to clean out your window wells," Roz said. "If there was a fire and anybody actually needed to escape through here, they'd kill themselves on all the garbage before the fire ever got to them."

I looked down into the window well. Some sort of vine wound around a twisted window screen, and a broken tree branch stared back at us, daring us to jump in and impale ourselves. I looked over at the row of poplars that ran along the back fence, and saw several other branches on the ground, poking up through the overgrown grass.

"He's letting the place go to hell," I said, a sick feeling in the pit of my stomach.

"This one is less lethal," Roz said. She'd moved over to the second window well. I came over and looked down. I didn't see anything but a bunch of slimy, rotting leaves and a couple plastic bags that had blown there, but I could well imagine the creepy-crawlies that might be living in the mulch.

"I hate to say it," I said, "but the other window might be easier—the screen is already out..."

Roz was easing herself into the leaf mold, which rose to well above her ankles. "Doesn't matter," she said, waving the metal strip. She was holding it by a plastic handle at one end, and it had a couple of weird notches at the other. "Screen is the easiest part."

"What is that, anyway?" I asked.

"Slim Jim."

"I thought those were for getting into cars."

She grinned up at me. "I used to sneak out of the house all the time during high school. My brother got sick of me waking him up to let me back in at two or three a.m., so he taught me how to get back in without getting caught."

With practiced ease that surprised me even though it probably shouldn't have, Roz pressed the Slim Jim along the edge of the screen, looking for just a hint of leverage. A moment later, it popped off. She set it aside.

She studied the dusty glass for a moment, then nodded as though she'd spotted whatever it was she'd been looking for. Sliding the Slim Jim along the window casing, she wiggled it a little to pry the glass away from the frame. Holding it steady with one hand, she snatched the crowbar from her belt-loop and pushed it into the opening she'd created between the two panes of glass.

"Don't break the window," I said, nervously dancing from foot to foot as I watched from above her.

"Have faith," she said. With a quick shove, I heard the cheap lock crack. Roz eased the crowbar back out and then wiggled the Slim Jim again to open a space wide enough for her fingers. "Ta da! One open window," she said, and slid the glass.

It scraped open about three inches and then stopped.

"There's probably a dowel blocking it," I said, in response to her puzzled frown.

"Woulda been nice if you'd mentioned that earlier," she grumbled, once again putting her Slim Jim skills to work. Gently prodding the glass open, she wiggled the thin strip of metal around, biting her tongue as she felt her way under the edge of the dowel and flipped it out of the way.

Withdrawing the Slim Jim, she slid the window the rest of the way open. "Okay, so not my best time, but we're in. Shall we get to work?"

"I always knew you'd lead me into a life of crime," I said, sitting down on the edge of the window well, and stretching my feet across the opening toward the window ledge. I did not want to step down into that leaf mold.

"Wuss," Roz said, helping me hoist myself in through the window without killing myself. She followed, sitting on the window ledge and dusting off her feet and legs before swinging them over onto the back of the couch that sat against the window. "Okay, you might have been justified," she said with a grimace, shaking the gunk off her gloved hands.

I stood in the middle of the room, a jumble of emotions washing over me. The room was filled with memories, of laughing children, family movie afternoons with their accompanying popcorn fights, and quiet evenings after the kids had been put to bed when Larry and I had danced to romantic music in the very spot where I was standing. A tear slid down my cheek.

I felt like a ghost, standing in this room, this house, the memories haunting me. I couldn't move, and could barely breathe.

Roz closed the window and replaced the dowel, then, when I still hadn't moved, came over and put her arm around me. "C'mon, kid," she said. "Reliving it will just make it harder. Let's go look at your picture—you need to get mad again."

I nodded, unwilling to trust my voice, and followed her up the half-flight of stairs to the combined kitchen-dining room on the main level. I closed my eyes to the clutter—and the happy crayon drawings covering the refrigerator—and went out into the living room.

The Picasso was there, in all its black-and-white glory, sitting on the narrow brick ledge above the charred black hole of the non-functional fireplace. The old chimney needed to be completely rebuilt to be up to code before a fire could be built safely, and that kind of expense had never been in the budget. Nor was the gas log we'd talked about installing instead. I'd filled the gap with a cheap little electric insert, but I'd taken it with me when I'd moved out, partly because I liked the cozy illusion from the fake flames, but mostly because the heating system in my apartment sucked.

"He didn't even hang it," I said, coming close enough to study the painting. "It's just sitting here."

"All the easier for us," Roz said, coming up behind me. She'd gone back out to the car, and now held the large, blanket-wrapped velvet painting I'd picked up over the weekend—I'd found it at a yard sale a few blocks from my neighborhood, and even the five bucks I paid had felt like too much at the time.

I pulled the package of Command Strips from my pocket. "I still want to hang this," I said, nodding toward the velvet.

"Absolutely," agreed Roz. "We can't have anyone accusing us of shoddy work." She leaned the wrapped painting against the sofa and went back to the dining area for a couple of sturdy chairs that we could stand on.

It took only a few minutes for us to replace the Picasso with the yard sale velvet and arrange a few knickknacks so it looked like we'd found the room that way. When we were finished, we stepped back and observed our work. A half-dozen dogs stared back at us from the dented wooden frame, a cheap, knock-off version of the classic "Dogs Playing Poker," populated with yapper-dog breeds instead of the tough mutts from the original.

"It's perfect," Roz said.

"Worth every penny," I said. "He loathes yapper-dogs."

My phone alarm bleeped. "Time to go. I've got to be back at work in fifteen," I said. "Can we swing through a drive-through on the way?"

"You got it," Roz said.

We wrapped the Picasso in the blanket and stowed it in the back of the car, locking the kitchen door behind us on our way out of the house.

I straightened my hair while waiting for an order of chili, fries, and a chocolate milkshake—hey, if I'm going to order fast food, it's going to be something I like—and we pulled up in front of my building with one minute to spare.

"I'll swing by your house later tonight to drop off the picture," Roz said.

"Can you hold onto it for a few days?" I asked, grabbing my lunch. "I want to let the accusations die down before I take it."

"Can do," she said. I closed the door and was heading up the walk when I heard the car horn blast behind me. I turned and Roz had powered down the passenger window and was beckoning for me to come back. It looked like she was holding something in her hand.

"What?" I said, hurrying back. "I'm out of time."

"Here." She thrust a small object toward me. It was a key.

"What's this—"

"They were on the rack by the kitchen door—looks like he had extras made. Thought you might like one, in case you ever needed to get back inside and didn't feel like going through a window."

I closed my hand around the key, gripping her hand at the same time. "Thanks," I said, words suddenly failing me.

"A little B&E every once in a while is good for the soul," she said with a laugh. "Now go on. It's after one."

"Call me later?"

"You bet. And I'll keep Picasso safe."

I stood there watching as Roz drove away, not caring any more about the time passing and my cooling lunch. I turned the key over in my hand and began to smile.

We'd tilted at a windmill, Roz and I, though it would be hard to say which of us was Quixote and which was Sancho in this particular escapade. And I knew Larry would flip a cog when he saw the switched-out painting, but I really didn't care.

The voices from the old, imagined conversation once again whispered in the back of my head.

Pablo, mon ami! Your sketch just arrived. It is perfect, exactly what I was hoping for. I cannot thank you enough!

You make too much of it, Louis. It is but a simple sketch. I am of the hope that your readers will like it, but in truth, it is almost certain to be quickly forgotten.

Not so, not so! I am no good predictor in the world of art, but I believe I can safely say that this sketch will resonate far more with people because of its simplicity than would a more complex work. Mark my words, Pablo, you have created something meaningful here. I want to be jealous, but you are my friend...

Tucking the key into my pocket, I turned and walked confidently into the building, ready to take on the world. The bright, bold sun that shone in the Picasso was shining on me, and I felt stronger than I had in a long time.

NOT GETTING AWAY WITH IT

MICHAEL WARREN LUCAS

Michael Warren Lucas's story "Not Getting Away With It" also deals with art, but in a completely different way from Lauryn Christopher's "Tilting at Windmills."

Michael has written more than 30 books, ranging from murder mysteries, technical tomes on Internet engineering, SF, and thrillers. He's best known for his crime and mystery novels, like git commit murder *and* Butterfly Stomp Waltz. *See all of Michael's books at mwl.io.*

About this story, he writes, "Go up to the northern three-fourths of my native Michigan, and everything is about tourism and the local artists. They're often combined, in tiny museums. Against that setting, I went looking for a heroine that was the exact opposite of my usual, with beliefs different than mine, in a place and time I would never put an adventure, for stakes utterly unlike my usual. Beth Stone hobbled in the door and whacked me with her cane. I'm sure I deserved it, even if we don't know why."

Beth Stone wondered how an eighty-two-year-old woman with enough osteoporosis to rival the Hunchback of Notre Dame had gotten herself into such a ridiculous place that she had no choice but to rob the village museum.

But here she was.

A sliver of midnight moon and the smeared light of the Milky Way offered just enough light for her to discern the Frayville Museum's pebbly white front walk. The black canvas satchel of tools in her left hand dragged at her shoulder, setting up an ache that'd last for days. Her hips felt pretty good tonight so she didn't truly need the wooden cane, but she used it to meticulously probe the path ahead before each step. Getting caught would be embarrassing, but shattering a femur during a robbery offered complete humiliation.

No, not complete.

A forged Matchpawn painting offered pride of place, for every tourist to see? *That* was complete humiliation.

Frayville couldn't afford a real Matchpawn—the whole blessed county didn't have the kind of money to buy even one of her grandfather's paintings, and Beth had willed both of hers to the Red Cross for the good work they did, but still, they could have hung a nice print or a reproduction or even just called it an *homage* to her magnificent ancestor.

But no.

And that foolish boy who ran the museum had proved he wasn't going to listen to her. Wouldn't admit that a woman could know better than he.

Far as Beth knew she was the only living person who had read Grandfather's diaries, filthy things that they were. They made it clear, he never would have painted an otter.

The painting in the museum wasn't merely a forgery—it was flat-out *fake*.

Even twenty years ago she would have jogged up to the museum's front door, confident that her lungs would work as well as the bellows over in the Children's Historical Museum, that her heart would trip-trip-trip along as it always had. Tonight she walked slowly, careful not to run out of air. When had her lungs grown so inflexible? She couldn't feel her pulse in her temples and wrists, the way she used to when she jogged down to the store, but tonight her heart rattled against her ribs in a way it never had before.

When had she gotten so *old?*

Old or not, she still loved Frayville. The breeze carried the heavy scent of feed corn almost desiccated enough to harvest, and just a hint of the healthy waters of Lake Huron only a mile away. People felt comfortable walking the sidewalks of an evening, not like those madhouse big cities. Maybe the City Council had needed to put speed bumps on the road into town to convince the tourists to slow down before State Road 861 turned into Frayville's Main Street, but they'd held the modern world at bay. CBS and NBC out of Flint carried out news of the world, the awful frame-up the liberals were doing on that noble President Nixon and the Russians having their own space station, but that only made Frayville all the more precious.

She could not let a young punk soil her beloved home with lies.

Or her famous—if privately flawed—ancestor with work he would not have done.

The museum's front door dated from the 1800s, a sturdy oak frame surrounding mullioned glass panes. Reflected moonlight showed how the glass had rippled and flowed in a hundred years. The bright girl that lived next door to Beth, the one who taught the sixth grade, what was her name? She'd said that glass was really a liquid, just a really thick one. Beth had laughed and said *isn't that the darndest thing* meaning it was wrong cause everyone knew glass was solid, but under that sliver moon dang if the old glass didn't look just like Plummer's Creek frozen mid-ripple.

Breaking it was going to be a shame, but burgling started with getting into the building. She had the masking tape and a hammer in her satchel, just like on Perry Mason and Ironsides, along with a couple other tools from Harold's garage, rest his soul.

Harold would have been a great help here.

Yes, he'd been a man, and like all men he had this need to Get Away With It. Grandfather Matchpawn's diaries had told her all she needed to know about men and their need to Get Away With It. But Harold had been satisfied by Getting Away With an extra beer on bowling night, not like Grandfather's shameful young ladies.

Harold would have spoken to that boy of a curator. Put him in his place right sharp.

If that hadn't worked, Harold would have handled tonight's business.

But Harold had been in his grave this last sixteen years. Beth herself had to save the truth about her grandfather.

The good truth, not the whole truth.

She should be home asleep—or, if not asleep, drifting on nature's cricket symphony. Perhaps counting their chirps to draw her to sleep, rather than counting *on* them to drown the tap of her cane on the dewy concrete walk.

Curator Tapper slept in the flat above the museum. Quiet was essential.

Best she finish this quickly and go home. A nice cup of herbal tea in front of a crackling fire, that was the thing. Sip chamomile and watch deceit in oil paint curl into ash. That'd put her right to sleep, the well-earned sleep of the righteous.

She'd seen the museum door countless times in her life, a dozen in the last week alone. It had a bolt just above her head and a lever handle that would have been the perfect height twenty years ago, before her spine began its corkscrew twist. If she taped up that one panel halfway between them, she should be able to push the lock-button on the handle and pull the bolt. The handle for sure. If she couldn't stretch her arm far enough around to pull the bolt, she'd have to take a second pane.

I have this, she hissed to her fluttering heart. Criminals break and enter all the time, and not even our brave boys in blue can catch them all. And criminals aren't that smart. I can out-think a criminal, especially when you see all their dirty tricks on Matlock.

Beth tugged the wide masking tape from her satchel and tore off a strip. First cover the pane with tape, then tap it with the hammer. The tape would muffle the sound of the glass breaking and would keep splinters from flying all over. That young curator wouldn't have any idea of how to pick up broken glass, not properly, and Beth didn't want any kids getting hurt.

Next to the pane of glass, the dangling strip of tape looked even skinnier. Covering the whole pane was going to take a whole mess of strips.

Maybe this was a bad idea?

No, she wouldn't let a spot of work put her off. Get in. Take the painting off the wall. Go home. Taping the windowpane was the most tedious, time-hungry part, but she'd get it done.

With both hands she pressed the tape into place. Yes, she'd need a good dozen strips to cover the whole pane. She let a hand drop to the lever handle while she fumbled for the roll of tape with the other.

The handle sagged under her.

Beth stopped, puzzled.

Not daring to trust her luck, she tugged the handle.

The door swung open. The faint creak barely penetrated the cricket chorus.

It was one thing to not lock your house—out here in the country, nobody locked their doors—but here? The City Council had entrusted Curator Tapper with their historical museum, and that fool couldn't be bothered to lock the door after hours?

He deserved to be robbed.

Once she resolved the matter of the false painting, she'd have to take it up with the City Council. If anonymous ruffians were going to pillage their treasures, the museum needed better locks.

Satchel in one hand and cane in the other, Beth hobbled into the darkness. The door shut behind her with a quiet click, shutting out the night breezes and insects and all Michigan's autumn glory and replacing it with a dusty mustiness that tickled her sinuses.

Beth gave her eyes a moment to adjust to the perfect blackness, but it stubbornly refused to ease. Grimacing, she fumbled in her satchel for the heavy flashlight. It ate those big blocky batteries but Harold had sworn by it and there's no chance she'd go against her husband's word.

The light splashed against the polished wood floor and cast a halo of light up through the museum. The high ceiling loomed, made mysterious by the inverted shadows of all the tables and display cases around Beth. She grimaced and clapped her hand over the flashlight lens, trying to block out some of the light before a passerby noticed the sudden illumination inside the museum. No, wait—the so-called curator might not have locked the door, but he had drawn the heavy drapes over the tall narrow windows and pulled the shade on the back of the door.

Nobody from outside would see a light.

Not even if she burned that loathsome painting right in the middle of the museum.

Cool your blood, missy. That was short-term thinking. A real Matchpawn would go for millions at auction. Everyone would think that the thief walked in the front door, scooped it up, and took it home. Even if they somehow suspected Beth and convinced a judge to search her home, they wouldn't find anything but perhaps a few ashes from the first fire of autumn.

Well-burned ashes.

Leaving the satchel right inside the door, she kept the flashlight low and hobbled up into the next room.

The Frayville Museum had been the home of Stuart Randall, mayor from 1880 through 1898, back in the days when folks dreamed of living long enough to see their grandparents. Beth knew Randall's story better than her own, how he'd brought in mining equipment and started pulling the best gypsum known to man out of Michigan's soil, just a couple miles from town. Once he'd made his fortune, Randall had hired master builders and craftsmen to assemble the finest building Frayville had ever seen. As a child Beth had studied the intricately decorated plaster ceilings to pick out the hidden faces. Those same eyes and mouths looked bloated and menacing in the reflected light, all gaping in horror and shock as she quietly snuck between the exhibits.

All she had to do now was not make noise. Don't wake Tapper, snug asleep on the floor overhead.

And there, at the back of the last room, hung the shameful painting.

A Matchpawn.

Thirty inches square, on canvas.

Beth had to admit that the forger had captured Grandfather's technique perfectly. The light reflected off the glossy wood floor exposed all the tiny brush-strokes and Grandfather's masterful palette of colors.

The painting hung above the abandoned fireplace in what had once been a dining room meant to hold a dozen people while leaving the servants room to gracefully bear their heavily loaded sterling silver serving platters. The placement let the painting loom over the delicate ceramics displayed throughout the room.

Ceramics! As if that was real art. Yes, Lucy Powliss had been a very skilled craftsman, and her little studio had brought good trade to Frayville, but plates and cups and bowls were utilitarian. They weren't real art, even if they could be dandied up.

And how incredible could Powliss be if she could leave all of these *unsold* pieces to her home town?

It was only right that a piece of real art, a Matchpawn no less, should lord over her lowly tradecraft.

If only the museum had chosen a real Matchpawn.

Instead, they had an otter.

Beth had read her grandfather's diaries more than once. The first time had been hard—once Grandmother had passed, he'd spent more pages on his assignations than on his craft, but still, he'd made his loathing of otters clear. They weren't even native to Michigan!

He would never have painted one.

Especially one looking so blasted... *cute*.

Cute was for children. Not serious art.

And Grandfather Matchpawn was nothing if not serious.

Beth hobbled forward, hurrying enough that she had to use her cane. All she had to do was knock the abomination down, drag it three blocks to her little house, and this shameful episode would vanish into Frayville's archives—

"I've been waiting for you, ma'am."

Beth twisted in surprise, the rubberized end of her cane almost popping off the floor.

Gawky Curator Tapper stood in the opposite doorway. He'd jammed his oversized plastic-rimmed glasses onto his face but hadn't taken the time to straighten them or comb his remaining hair. His bathrobe hung misaligned on his shoulders, the sash knotted in a lopsided bow. The light reflecting off the floor gave his features an unnatural cast, his nose casting a shadow up between his eyes and making his mouth a dark pit.

Beth's innards plunged, her heart lurching into higher gear like the big trucks trying to get up one of the steep hills of M-23 even as her brain ground to a halt.

"Not even going to say hello, Missus Stone?"

She'd been silent.

If she panicked, the whole town would know.

She had to convince Tapper, and convince him now.

"You have a duty." Beth hated how her voice had grown thinner and more reedy over the decades. She tried to will gravitas into her tone. "The city entrusted you with our history. You are here to safeguard it, not shill us with lies."

"Missus Stone," Tapper shook his head. "We've been through this. I swear to you, that is a real Matchpawn. By your grandfather. Painted on his 1891 trip to Vancouver."

"It's not in his diaries!" Beth snapped.

"Which you've been most definite about not letting anyone else read."

Beth clamped her teeth. He'd mentioned the otters in the diaries, yes—he'd called them "insipid, much like my companion Charity, but the latter possessed of much greater intimate charms." Aloud Beth said, "And wouldn't you, and every one of those danged professors, just love to dig through his personal thoughts?"

"We all would," Tapper said. "He was a great artist."

"This is a fake!" Beth jerked a rheumatic finger up at the offending painting. "You won't even have it sent to a specialist to check it. Foolish boy."

"I'm fifty-three—" Tapper shook his head and pulled off his glasses to rub his eyes.

"If the city council won't make you fix this disrespectful lie, then I have no choice." Her voice still sounded too querulous, as she had doubt. Curse this mortal shell.

Tapper pushed his glasses back onto his face, taking the extra half-second to align them correctly. "Listen. Missus Stone. It came authenticated."

"It was in the New York Times interview," Beth said. "August twelfth, eighteen ninety-six. 'Nature is God's majesty and grace incarnate, and it is my duty to bring that to the people. Charming is for children, and I do not paint for children.'" She shook her hand at the otter. "And that, sir, is nothing but charming."

Tapper closed his eyes and slowly shook his head. "I can see you're on top of things."

"I might be old, but I'm not daft! Not yet."

"All right, then. All right." Tapper's mouth twisted, but with a sudden charge as quick as flicking a light switch his face erupted into a cocky grin. "You know, I think I'll tell you what's really going on."

"What's going on is that you're an idiot," Beth said.

"That painting's a total fake. Nicely forged, if I do say so myself."

Beth stopped.

Whatever she'd expected, it hadn't been that.

"You know?"

"Of course I know!" Tapper raised his spread hands and let his smile swell. "That's not the best part. The best part is..." He leaned his head a little forward, as if trying to see her more closely without moving his feet. "The best part is, every single item in this museum is a fake."

"Ridiculous! I've been on the heritage committee for almost forty years, since before you were born!"

"I'm fifty-three."

"Whatever!"

"Didn't anyone on the committee ever wonder how you attracted an actual curator to your museum? To work for a pittance and a flat?" Tapper giggled—the man actually *giggled*. "Because piece by piece, I've replaced every exhibit with a forged duplicate and sold the original."

"Oh, don't give me that story," Beth said.

Still grinning, Tapper plucked up one of Powliss' oh-so-haughty ceramic dinner plates to hold it beside his head. "This plate? I can order them from Japan, just like this."

"Stop this foolishness."

Tapper brought his arm down in a single sweeping crash.

The sound of ceramic shattering against the corner of the table echoed through the museum.

Beth's breath froze in her throat.

"I know you're upset," Tapper said. "But please don't break any more ceramics, Missus Stone."

Beth knew that expression. She'd seen it on the face of every young man in town. Boys had a time when they thought nothing really bad could happen to them, that they could run and jump and even leap off Dead Moose Rock into Lake Huron without getting hurt. Life eventually abraded away that certainty, unless a boy broke a leg or a back or a neck and all the others caught a whiff of the Reaper brushing past.

Even in her grandfather's diaries, every encounter he'd written of with a young lady had dripped with certainty.

Her Harold only had a little touch of the look, and only once in a while. A beer didn't rate much of a victory.

But Tapper's grin carried a whole bunch of repressed Getting Away With It.

The sight set fury sizzling down Beth's nerves.

"It's amazing," Tapper said. "There's nothing like a really great con, you know? Once I have the last few bits replaced, I'll just..." He waved a hand. "Fade away."

Pillaging her town's museum? Stripping one of the decent spots in the world? "I can't believe—nobody's so greedy!"

Tapper laughed. "It's not for the money. Not just about the money." His face lost its humor. "It's the joy of craft. Your grandfather painted. Miss Powliss cast ceramics. And I... my craft, my joy, what lights up my soul?" He stepped closer. The inverted illumination made his face not only macabre, but menacing. "Fraud, my dear Miss Stone. And it's so very rare that I get to tell *anyone* about it."

Beth knew what that meant. It was the sort of thing the kidnappers said before "disposing" of their victims, though why the TV shows wouldn't just say "murder" she was sure she never understood.

And he was going to blame her for ceramics that *he'd* busted up.

Fortunately, she was far too angry to be afraid.

"Perhaps that's why I had the painting made," Tapper said. "So I could finally tell someone."

As if Beth could care about why he'd committed such a crime. She shifted her cane and took a step sideways, bringing her right up against a display table. "I have one thing to say to you, young man."

"Oh?" The smile returned. "And what is that?"

While Tapper waited for her to speak, she shifted the heavy flashlight to shine right in his face.

Tapper shouted and raised an arm to protect his vision.

Beth dropped the cane, snatched a priceless Powliss ceramic off the table, and flung it straight at Tapper.

By the time it sailed past his head, the second and third cups were airborne. The second bounced off his stomach, but the third ricocheted off his forehead into his raised arm and back into his shadowed face.

Tapper shouted in surprise, maybe in pain.

Ceramic crashed against the floor.

Beth stepped forward to snatch at a stack of saucers, hurling them two at a time. "How dare you!"

Tapper jerked his hands protectively out in front of his face. "Stop it, you crazy bitch!"

"I'm crazy?" She grabbed a serving bowl but its weight yanked it out of her hand when she tried to lift it, so she snatched at a gracefully curved gravy boat instead. "Crazy is thinking you could steal my town's past!"

The gravy boat hit Tapper square on the chin.

He staggered in surprise. One bare foot came down on an unbroken teacup, which shot out from under and took the whole foot with it, throwing his whole body back.

The sound of Tapper's head hitting the floor made Beth wince.

She'd only gotten twelve, maybe fifteen good whacks in with her cane before the police arrived.

Beth was angry enough to chew tin cans and spit nails. They'd put her in the back of the police car, where the criminals went, where it smelled of bleach and puke and damp. *Her* on the sticky ragged vinyl seat, not the charlatan Tapper.

If Tapper was even his real name.

That young officer (whatever his name was) stayed in the car with her, but he wouldn't even take a proper statement. He'd stopped writing everything down hours ago, and he'd just kept nodding and yes, ma'am-ing her like she was a child that wouldn't shut up even though Beth kept saying what that lying liar had told her.

Exhaustion weighed her down. Her every joint hurt. Her back ached from the tip of her tailbone up to the crown of her skull. She'd gotten used to the odd white night, when sleep evaded her, but she'd never before gone burgling. Throwing all that cutlery and wielding her cane had sapped her strength. Only indignation kept her up.

And a "silent alarm?" Who had ever heard of such a thing?

The sun had started to stain the eastern sky pink before Sergeant Fox trudged out of the museum's front entrance. The boy babysitting her perked up. "About time," Beth said. "I've known Sergeant Fox since he was a boy. Maybe *he'll* listen to me."

"I sure hope so, ma'am."

"Don't you get fresh with me, young man."

"I wouldn't dream of it, ma'am."

The police car rocked as Sergeant Fox eased his bulk behind the wheel. "Missus Stone. Have you calmed down?"

"I am the picture of calm, Sergeant Fox." Beth struggled to straighten her spine, despite her exhaustion. "As always."

"Yeah." Stone raised a hand to rub his forehead. "Listen to me, ma'am. Mister Tapper could press charges if he wanted."

"Charges? Whatever for? He's the criminal!"

"Assault."

"I never laid a hand on him!"

"Your cane is a deadly weapon, ma'am."

"That's a highly backwards way to look at things, young man." She could feel the anger driving her words, but felt too tired to pull its reins. Once the anger ran out, she'd collapse. "You need to remember who changed your diapers."

"That's how I persuaded him to not press charges," Fox said.

"I should hope so."

"Instead, we're going to have Doc Smythe check you out."

Beth scowled. "If I wasn't fit, could I have given that cheat what he so plainly deserved?"

"What did you think you were doing?" Fox said.

"I've explained it all to your young man, but he's simply not listening."

"But I had to deal with Mister Tapper while you did that." Fox's face tightened. "I knew I could trust you to behave. You've been here your whole life."

Was he really trying to sweet-talk her? "You're no better at sweet-talking than your boy here."

"Ma'am." Fox's teeth were clamped together. "What. Were you. Doing. Here. Tonight?"

"Getting rid of that forgery. He even admitted it was a fake."

Fox glanced at the younger officer. Once the kid nodded Fox said, "Did you throw all those cups and saucers at the curator, then hit him with your cane?"

"He threatened to do away with me." Even as she spoke, she realized how pathetic she sounded.

Fox heaved out a breath. "Here's what's going to happen. I'm going to take you home. Doc Smythe will be by this morning to do his exam. We'll decide from there."

Beth found the strength to clamp her own mouth shut.

What could she say?

She could say how Tapper had confessed to scamming Frayville, and sound like a feeble old lady. The best that would happen? Pitying looks all around town. She remembered all too well being in her thirties and forties and fifties, all too sure that she wouldn't end up that way, but everyone did. The Reaper came for all, but when he was in a mood he started with the mind.

Even if she was one day vindicated, she didn't have time to waste.

She had proof that the painting was forged, in Grandfather's sadly unexpurgated diaries that only she had read. What was she supposed to do, get a black market and scratch out all the naughty bits? There wouldn't be much diary left!

And she was old.

Tired.

Maybe she'd go down fighting...

...but maybe, this far into her life, she'd lose.

Beth sagged back in her seat. "Fine. I'll stay home and wait for Doc."

Fox started the engine. "Good girl."

Beth's hair stuck to the seat when she turned her head. She'd have to take a bath before she could sleep just to get the police car off of her, and get an appointment with Abbie to get her hair totally redone.

The museum's outdoor lights were on, showcasing the sturdy red brick walls.

Tapper stood at the front door, holding something white to his head. A towel, maybe? Wrapped around ice? Good.

Tapper's shoulders drooped—no, his whole face drooped. He look aggrieved and confused, as if he couldn't understand how someone could do him so wrong. His picture could go in the dictionary right next to *misery*.

His eyes met hers.

The man's mouth twitched.

That Getting Away With It smile ghosted across his face, and vanished.

A second later, the police car lurched into gear.

Beth settled back into the seat to ease her aches.

She really wanted that bath.

But maybe she'd call that art history professor from Michigan State University first. That one who'd been so insistent about Grandfather Matchpawn's diaries.

And if she had to choose between protecting her village now, for all the folks who lived here today, or protecting her long-dead grandfather, well, that wasn't much of a choice, now was it?

Informing young Tapper he was *not* Getting Away With It would be an added pleasure.

WITH THIS RING

DAVID STIER

We go from the near-history of Michael Warren Lucas's "Not Getting Away With It," to a time that all of us think of as actual history. Army veteran David Stier, who served in Germany during the Cold War, has a passion for history. He's visited many Civil War battlefields, including Fredericksburg, where this story is set.

The inspiration for this story came from David's research. He writes, "The Battle of Fredericksburg was a bloody defeat for the Union, but a situation map of the battle revealed one area on the left flank in which the Union advanced significantly under the command of General George Meade of Gettysburg fame. This advance as portrayed in this story probably would have succeeded had not General Franklin failed to reinforce the breakthrough. After more research on the participating regiments, this tale emerged."

David's fiction has appeared in eight volumes of Fiction River, *most recently in* Doorways to Enchantment. *His work has also appeared in* Pulphouse Magazine. *A collection of his World War II stories,* Final Solutions: Stories of the Holocaust, *just appeared.*

David's historical fiction is so vivid that it almost seems as if he lived through each of these battles. Settle in and prepare yourself for "With This Ring."

Fredericksburg, Virginia, 13 December, 1862

Ex-corporal Robert Bowles, along with the rest of the First Pennsylvania Reserves, stood facing southwest in line of battle. He looked from left to right. The other regiments were still forming up.

He hefted his cartridge box, checking he had enough ammunition. The dull rattle-comfort of Minie balls helped quiet the all-overish dread. He undid the flap and checked some of the paper cartridges.

Last night after sundown the weather had froze. That and the fog made for a miserable night. Dratted fog sometimes had a mind to foul powder too. Not this time though.

Next he checked his haversack's dry rations, then the canteen. He'd learned the hard way not to tote no more than that. Satisfied, he made sure his bayonet was secure in its scabbard then stooped over and re-tied his Brogans. No call to trip on loose shoelaces. Body'd like to end up dead meat that way. Finally, he re-secured his Ketchum grenade. Usually useless as tits on a boar, but when they did work they was a pyrotechnic delight.

The lackadaisical manner of the other regiments was a sore trial indeed. Morning fog was thinning fast now. Why hadn't they pushed off at 7:00 'stead of 9:00 when the fog still coated the fighting ground? Might've made it a ways up Prospect Hill afore the Reb cannon cut loose.

"Just a quick jaunt tomorrow boys," Colonel McCandless had told the assembled brigade last night. "Cross lots through those stubble fields then mosey on up that bitty hill. Surprise the graybacks with a warm Pennsylvania how-do. Flank ol' Bobby Lee and take 'em from the rear. What say you to that?"

The *huzzahs* had been poorer than Job's turkey and the colonel had been hard pressed to carry his tune any further. But somewhat he managed. Wouldn't been a colonel, else.

Well, in the fast-thinning fog, that hill looked all-mighty steep. Would get even steeper once Johnny's cannons began their tune; for sure as Jesus beat the Dutch, Rebel cannon was aimed on 'em right now. And when they cut loose, that cross lots little jaunt might turn into a race to perdition.

That speech hadn't fooled no one 'cept maybe the 121st Pennsylvania, who'd not yet seen the elephant. Couple hours, give or take, and that would change.

Bowles turned, looked at the rookie regiment, spied those that he could see. Yup. Round eyes, white faces, an occasional swipe of a sweaty palm across a sweaty forehead, probably a few puking their guts as well. Nothing to be shamed of neither, for he'd done it too, way back when. He spit off to the side.

So much for speechifyin' colonels.

His gaze moved to the left. James Shields, his one-time best friend, smiled and blew him a kiss. A couple of Shields's mates saw and snickered. Bowles' hand tightened on the barrel of his Springfield. He tried not to scowl but from Shields's grin he knew he'd failed. And that served only to cross Bowles even more. He glanced from Shields to his missing stripes then spit some chaw Shields's way, wiped his mouth, looked a mite on the ring Sarah'd give him last week. Why he kept it was another puzzle. Bowles wondered if she still wore the one he'd give her. Probably not, considering.

All their lives, Shields had come out on top. Whether at the annual turkey shoot or harvest dance, it was Shields who'd bagged the biggest bird or the most after-dance kisses—sometimes more than kisses, too.

When Sarah'd chose him 'stead of Shields, Bowles had stood there, mouth agape, like the town drunk all wallpapered for fair and too numbed to reply. But then he'd took her in his arms and they'd kissed for the first time as betrothed.

He'd give anything not to have saw Shields kissin' Sarah later that same night. Shields's black eye and mashed lips from the two fights they had yesterday somewhat eased the rage. But for damn sure not near enough.

She'd the right to choose and Bowles was man enough to take her choice, but why'd she say yes to him first then let Shields do what he'd done?

A nagging thought surfaced, one he'd had several times since returning to camp ahead of Shields. What had he really saw? Sarah wasn't no fancy girl. She'd not act that way after taking Bowles's ring and Bowles taking hers. Shields liked touring the bawdy houses 'round Washington and maybe that's what Sarah wanted—but that made no sense neither. Did it?

Maybe listening to Shields 'stead a tryin' to whup him was the road to take. They'd knowed each other since they was five. More than once since Sumter they'd trusted each other with their lives. His gut flipped-flopped like he'd just jumped off a cliff. Did he even deserve Sarah's love? He'd knowed her just as long. It weren't Shields who'd throwed the first punch yesterday morning, neither.

He stared long and hard at Shields's grinning face. Shields finally looked away, started joshing with the man next. Bowles spit again. Some couldn't get enough of Shields's falderal.

Ah, hell. Bowles kicked a clod of mud. Maybe a certain ex-corporal would end up cold as a wagon tire this day. Maybe for the best and no great shakes if so.

Bowles nodded to the new man—Jessup—standing in the next file. Jessup nodded back.

"Been down this road afore, have ya?" Bowles asked. Word was that Jessup had survived a bad 'un at Second Bull Run. Survived the hospital too, which took even more grit. Bowles noted the mushed Minie ball looped 'round Jessup's neck on a gold chain.

"Yup," Jessup said, "been down this road afore. Hope to stay on it till we hit Richmond."

Bowles nodded again, cut off a plug of tobacco, offered it, then cut another for hisself. "God willing and the creek don't rise might see us both there together."

The drums sounded from the rear.

"Forward men!" one of the new nameless lieutenants yelled in a high-pitched voice. "For God and country and Honest Abe!"

Bully for you sir and damned lucky if yer still kickin' tonight. Fresh fish lieutenants passed through the regiment like the Virginia quick-step shot out one's arse after drinking green beer. The officer *huzzahed* again and waved his saber in the air. Bowles and Jessup both spit a stream of tobacco juice, guffawed as one. Yup, Jessup had sure 'nough been down this road afore.

Bowles and the rest of the First Pennsylvania crossed the Richmond stage road, advancing for about an hour under warming clear blue skies. No graybacks. No Minie ball hornets *whizzing* by. Too damn quiet. Then he spied a 20-foot long dark streak headed his way. He hit the muddy wheat-stubbled field, covered his head with an arm. The *flying lamppost* passed overhead, followed seconds later by a gut-cutting *screech*. Too close by far, the solid cannon shot—easy to reckon from the pug-ugly wail—hit a few yards to his right.

He watched a blue-sleeved arm as it spun skyward, a faint red sheen spraying in a circular fan. Nearby screams earmarked another cripple, or soon-to-be corpse. The mingled stench of cordite, sweat, and blood made Bowles sneeze. Another solid shot *whizzed* by.

The din of cannon, cursing, and wounded, failed to keep his mind on the present situation. That was bad. Them who didn't keep at least a step ahead, most like ended up dead. He shook his head, trying to clear the cobwebs and maybe rattle some sense into the last few days, but he couldn't get Shields and Sarah's kissing out of his noggin.

Another *lamppost* blurred by and more screams commenced.

The reaped wheat stubbles dug into his belly and legs. Right nice accommodations though. Still breathing meant being cozy as could be. Damn Johnny's definitely had the range. Bowles scrambled to his feet and ran for a middling sized ditch a ways ahead. A few paces on he knelt and slapped the new lieutenant on the back.

"Forward, sir!" Bowles encouraged the fuzz-faced officer. "Forward for God and country!"

He glimpsed a youngish white face and terror-goggled eyes, like the boy had just seen Sam Hill hisself. Bowles rushed on with a wild cackle that at least kept the screams of the wounded at bay. The lieutenant lunged up and lurched after him, waving his saber above his head.

"Come on boys! Follow me!" The lieutenant's voice cracked. Most within earshot rushed forward with a ragged cheer.

Another wailing *screech*. Bowles flattened again, along with all the old hands, fifty yards closer to that wonderful blessed ditch. How in hell could a single cannon cause so much misery? Best yet, where in blazes was their own counter-battery?

He rolled over onto his back. The lieutenant, still standing, waved his saber and urged men on to the attack.

"Get down sir!"

The youngun's face registered a faint relief, as though he could parcel his courage away for a time, but too late, the officer's kepi and top of his head disappeared. He stood motionless for a few seconds, eyes rolling skyward then he slumped to hands and knees. What was left of his brains quivered within the uncapped skull. Blood streamed to earth from the jagged opening. This time Bowles got more than a whiff of blood.

The lieutenant raised his head. Their eyes met afore the life faded and he slumped forward, butt poised in a strange parody of the hill they'd yet to reach. Not proper, that, so Bowles crawled over and laid the man out on his back. Might've made a good officer had Providence been less spare. Man deserved a measure of respect for the grit he'd showed, too.

Some of the boys broke and fled. Another shot passed overhead and even more skedaddled. Bowles wiped sweat from his brow, cursed the sun and heat. Damned Reb weather. Freeze your arse off all night, sweat it off all day.

Coarse frightened voices now joined the screams of the wounded. The shit smell of men who'd voided then died worked on his nose, itching it something fierce. Finally, he sneezed, crouched, and headed again for that ditch. From the corner of his eye he spied someone else making for the same spot. He jumped over the lip and slid down the side, landing in a cold puddle of smelly black water.

Seconds later, the other Pennsylvanian slid alongside, drenching them both in a muddy sheet.

"Grand aim, my friend," Bowles said. "Couldn't a done better mysel—"

"It would have to be you, I reckon," said Shields, a dark frown plastered across his pan.

Bowles inched back up to the top of the ditch, peered over the edge. To the rear, the rest of the regiment lay stuck. The Union cannon had finally let rip but from the dark puff-balls appearing over the Federal regiments, some of the fuses were cooking off early, raining shrapnel onto their own troops. This here frolic had all the earmarks of another cocked hat fix.

He and Shields were a hundred yards past the next closest rank and file. Till that Reb cannon got spiked, the boys would be staying right where they was.

To the front, the railroad stretched from northeast to southwest in a lazy S that hugged the base of several hills. Straight ahead a dense forest of skinny, close-spaced spruce carpeted the slopes of Prospect Hill. To the west he spied the tallest roofs of Fredericksburg; above which was a powerful steep slope, and what looked like a stretch of stone wall running its length.

He took a swig of water. General Meade's boys—Bowles included —mayhap had drawn the better hand with this southern flanking attack. Plain and simple, that stone wall looked like death. Plugging any Federals that moseyed up that rise would be like shooting a line of toy ducks at the county fair.

Last night after the second fight with Shields, Bowles had heard music floating from Fredericksburg proper, the faint sounds of several pianos carrying on the wind. He'd heard that General Sumner's troops had looted the town. Must've decided a little entertainment would soothe their *savagerous* souls afore the battle. Damned lunkheads. The Rebs had eyes and ears too, and some of those boys most like had kin in these parts. Stunt like that would serve only to sharpen the aim all along that stone wall.

Another round of shot whistled in from the left flank. Bowles glimpsed the smoke that blossomed up and out from a shallow cut near a crossroads well forward of the grayback lines.

He slid back down to Shields's side.

"Our cannon's firing at the wrong damn piece a ground," he said.

Shields smiled—at least with his mouth, but the eyes held that down-yer-nose hobnobery that Bowles knew so well.

"Added foretelling to yer list a talents, have ya?" Shields said. "A private's what ya are now, jus' like me, so's let our cannon do their job for a spell."

Bowles scowled. Shields returned the favor with a malicious leer. Bowles' free hand formed a fist while the other leaned his rifle against the ditch.

"The Johnnies 've unlimbered a single gun 'bout a hundred yards left a here. The enfilading fire's comin' from there," Bowles said.

"Boy howdy," Shields said. "Privates ain't supposed ta use such high-falutin words."

Bowles grabbed Shields by the blouse, pulled his face to within an inch of his own.

"Them's our fellas catching it back there, you piss proud little whoremonger. Don't know 'bout you, but I aim to lend a hand. Might hate yer guts fer what ya did with Sarah, but I never took ya fer no coward."

Shields pushed hisself free. "Whoremonger is it? Some horizontal refreshment might a helped you an Sarah both, ya jealous son of a bitch." Shields reached into his blouse. "Been tryin' to give ya this here letter since I got back an all's ya want to do is pound my noggin. From Sarah it is. She cried long hours after ya left." He swiped at Bowles's ring finger. "Serve ya right if she ask back that ring."

Letter? Why'd Sarah send him a letter after what he'd caught her and Shield's a doin'? He looked long and hard at Shields's angry face, wanting him to look away so's he could see the lie.

A solid shot hit the edge of the ditch, half-burying Bowles in wet dirt.

He scrambled free, ears ringing, nose registering the smell of cordite and black dirt. He reached back into the ditch, grabbed his rifle. Looked to be undamaged, few more scratches was all. No sign of Shields. Hightailed it? Then he remembered the letter. Another damned lie, most like.

Bowles made for the Johnny 12-pounder a ways farther left. Another round cut loose, leaving a tell-tale smoke ring which vanished after traveling a few yards. Union gunners couldn't spy her 'cause of it being in that cut.

WITH THIS RING

A ramrod swung up and over a high bush. Bowles froze in place. A few seconds later another solid shot *whizzed* by. Bowles bellied back to a stand of sturdy oak. Once there, he climbed high enough to spy the graybacks from a branch growing straight out from the trunk, a nice perch and a solid spot for reloading. Best yet, the thick trunk served as cover.

Twenty-five yards away, the cannon's crew scuttled round like ants on a hot griddle. Behind the 12-pounder, an officer urged the gunners on. Plugging an officer would feel right nice, but there was bigger fish to fry in that there little hole. Bowles unslung his rifle, rested the barrel in the Y of a branch, aimed at the lead gunner instead.

As the Reb readied to light off the next round, Bowles fired. A second later the gunner took a stumbling step backward and slumped to the ground.

Loud cursing rose from the rest. They looked round like a peck of skeared hens. Bowles ducked, re-loaded, took aim and fired again. A second Johnny fell and lay still. The rest of the graybacks scattered for cover. He reloaded, cocked the hammer again, figuring to take out a few more afore skedaddling.

A faint metallic click sounded to his rear.

"Hey Yank, get somethin' for *y,all* now, boy," said a voice that had as much in common with Pennsylvania as Jeff Davis had with John Brown.

Before Bowles could turn, a shot echoed. He flinched, expecting a Minie ball to do him up proper, but a thump, rattle, and groan was what he got instead.

Ten feet from his tree, a Johnny in homespun butternut lay sprawled on his side, the ground round his chest blackening in a pool of blood. Shields, squatting halfway between the ditch and Bowles, raised one hand, middle finger extended, his face again plastered with that down-yer-nose hobnobery smile.

Lord how I hate that goddam smile.

A red tinged rage focused on Shields's face. Bowles hand tightened on the stock and without meaning to his finger pulled the trigger. The Springfield jumped in his hands. A look of surprise crossed Shields's face and he clutched his chest with his left hand as he fell backwards with a blood stain growing round his heart. Bowles stared at his rifle and the smoke curling from its muzzle.

What 'uv I done? Didn't mean ta shoot...

Shields raised his right arm, clutching something white and bloodstained in his hand for a few seconds afore the arm fell, lifeless, to the ground.

A Minie ball *thunked* into the tree near Bowles's noggin. He turned back toward the 12-pounder as several more followed. He reloaded his rifle as the graybacks rushed to reposition the gun. The mile-wide seeming muzzle left no doubt as to the next target. Bowles fired again and another grayback fell.

He climbed down from the tree, Minie balls hurrying him on. He tried to reach Shields while bullets followed him like a nest of angry hornets. He made a last attempt to reach Shields, but the fallen tree he used as cover shook from even more rifle fire. A splinter of wood lanced his check in fiery pain. He unlimbered his grenade and rushed the cannon, closing the distance then lobbing the dart-shaped contraption as hard as he could in a high arc. Even more Minie balls *whizzed* by but none hit him. The grenade landed next to the ammo limber and exploded, for once doing its job. The exploding gunpowder knocked him down, concussion squeezing his head that sent his ears to ringing something fierce. The gunners all looked to be dead but not the riflemen close by who somehow kept missing, but they did keep Bowles from reaching Shields.

Bowles legged it back towards his regiment, the *hiss* of Minie balls sounding even more like a growing passel of angry hornets. One holed his kepi, which he scooped up without breaking stride. All the way back to his lines, Bowles tried to deny what had happened, but the surprise on Shields's face and the blood around his heart put paid to that lie.

Several of the boys looked his way and cheered. Bowles glanced back at a huge pall of smoke. While he was congratulated and back-slapped he tried to act happy. A real hero who'd saved the day.

But all's he could think about was Shields's raised arm falling in death.

"*Huzzah*, boys!" screamed Capt. Fager, saber in one hand, Navy Colt in the other, as he led the charge up Prospect Hill. "We've breached their lines! What say we settle their hash for good this time?"

The company cheered and charged up slope, firing their Springfields as though possessed. Bowles screamed as loud as the rest, allowing battle rage to take him a far piece away so's not to think on Shields. He knelt, aimed, and plugged a grayback picket dumb enough to raise his head. He reloaded then continued on, screaming even louder. From the few scattered shots directed their way, it sure 'nough looked like they'd breached the grayback lines. Cordite and ripening bodies worried at Bowle's nose and sweat stung his eyes, so he wiped it away with a sleeve.

After he'd made it back to the company, Captain Fager congratulated him for fair.

"Bully piece of work, Bowles. The Colonel said you've just won back those stripes plus one more."

"More 'n likely a wood overcoat, too. Hey, Bobby-Boy?" said one of Shields's friends. Upon his return and when he was asked about Shields by the same man, Bowles gut flip-flopped and he almost puked his guts, but managed at the last moment to swallow both the vomit and bile.

"He took a Minie ball in the chest," Bowles said in a version of the truth that sent a shiver down his back. He tried to sound sad, but the lie didn't take with most of 'em —'specially the ones who'd knowed 'bout Bowles being jealous over Shields and Sarah. His pan probably gave the lie too. Shields had always said he was no good at cards 'cause his face gave it all away.

A Minie ball *whizzed* by his head with the hollow *hornet-buzz* they made when they came that close. Gave a body some warning, but the voice in his head asked if that was a good or bad thing.

A wounded horse lay across Bowle's path. He skirted the poor beast whose lower jaw had been blowed off. One shattered leg—the white blood-spattered bones a rank sight alongside its mud-caked body. Stale horse sweat and loamy smelling shit surrounded Bowles in a gut rumbling vice.

The animal blinked an eye as he passed, took in a ragged breath and tried to stand. Bloody snot shot from its nose then it settled back onto its side, sucked in several shallow breaths and held his gaze with what looked like a plea.

He knelt alongside the beast's head, pulled out his bayonet, ran it quickly through the eye and into the brain. It shuddered once then lay still. Maybe a Reb horse, but it hadn't asked for this here war. As he moved on the pleading look in the horse's eye was replaced with Shields's look of surprise. Bowles shook his head, once more trying and failing to erase his crime.

Then he noticed dead horses scattered all over the hill. Some had their bellies ripped open, the guts stretched out in slick grayish ropes. One headless specimen stood on all fours, a shattered tree propping it up. Not many dead soldiers, though, on either side. Place looked like a bivouac. Mayhap they *was* in the grayback rear. Bowles moved toward the dead Johnny he'd just plugged, wiped his bayonet on the man's blouse then continued uphill.

More evidence of a breakthrough appeared. Stacked rifles. Knapsacks piled near collapsed tents. Next to another dead horse lay a dead Reb general, least it looked so from the gobs of chicken guts stitched on his sleeves and collar. He'd taken one in the spine down low, probably a quick painless death. Up ahead, voices raised in a ragged cheer. As he reached a group of milling Federals, he spied a column of graybacks hightailing it for the rear. The boys sent 'em on with a few well-placed shots, but Bowles had already done enough killing this day.

An one that can't never be took back.

Someone passed him a jug of corn liquor. He took a hefty swig, then another, followed by a third.

"What's happenin'?" he asked the jug-passer.

"We caught 'em napping for a change," the man said, wiping his mouth with a sleeve. "Most of them's rifles was stacked when we made their camp so they skedaddled. Have some more, friend. This tanglefoot's the real deal." He threw back his head and brayed. "We finally whupped ol' Bobby Lee!"

Bowles took another hefty swig, passed the jug on back. About time to find what's left of the company, he reckoned. He spied the captain and headed that way. As he neared the crowd, someone slapped Bowles on the back, said: "Well, *Sergeant*, what's it feel like to be a high-falutin hero?"

Bowles' pride at spiking the Reb cannon changed to the surprised look on Shields's face—a vision that would never leave him or never erase what he'd done. He squared his shoulders, tried keeping his pan blank as he looked again at his rifle, expecting it to somehow reveal the truth. Now that the fighting was over, it seemed he had more in league with the Rebs. Again Shields's right arm and clenched fist with the bloodstained letter rose and fell inside Bowles's head. Knowing the lie, he kept telling hisself that the one path he had left laid with Sarah's letter. Bowles clutched that straw now, hoping it would somehow erase the stain on his soul.

"Okay, boys," Colonel McCandless galloped up, bellowing loud enough to quiet those close by. "We ain't finished yet, not by a country mile. The graybacks're still out there and we've got to stay on their tails. So let's—"

A red stain appeared on the hind-quarters of the colonel's horse. It reared with a whinny, turned and careened back down Prospect Hill toward the Federal lines. The colonel held on, looking a far piece less dignified then he had seconds afore.

Several of the boys screamed, spun, and fell. The sound of massed rifle fire echoed across the overrun Rebel camp. Another volley sent more Federals to the ground. A chorus of grayback Minie balls started ushering the Federals all back the way they'd come.

Up slope the rising din of Rebel yells from hundreds, mayhap thousands of Southern throats ended the Federal advance.

Johnny cannon fire sent canister shot into the retreating Federal ranks. Bowles joined in the headlong retreat, his crime forgotten for now as survival took to the fore. As Minie balls whistled by, he more than half hoped at least one of 'em would put paid to his coward's act.

Bowles crept back up Prospect Hill, the Virginia fog he'd cussed the night afore now an ally. He thanked this small measure that Providence had spit up.

The Johnnies—some said Stonewall Jackson's boys—had come screaming down Prospect Hill like the devil hisself was on their side. They'd rolled up the Federal advance in short order, sending them all hightailing it back the way they'd come.

The retreating Federals had gone down like wheat afore a reaper. They'd finally stopped the graybacks near the Richmond Stage Road. The fighting within the forest had been mostly hand to hand. Stonewall had tried to turn the retreat into a rout, but massed Federal cannon fire had broke his line instead. Bowles spit a plug of chaw to the frozen ground. They'd reaped a small measure of their own with that, at least.

For all intents, the southern wing of this battle was over. Bowles had heard of horrendous losses above Fredericksburg at a place named Marye's Heights. There was talk of another try tomorrow. The memory of that stone wall glimpsed earlier floated up inside his head along with Shields's raised right arm and Bowles shuddered.

Word here was to dig in and hold. The graybacks seemed to agree, least after their last charge, they'd melted back within the woods and it had been quiet ever since.

His stomach knotted and his heart hammered. Fog clung to the ground. The dense forest reminded him of happier times when he and Shields had hunted in the Pennsylvania woods. So far he'd been lucky and hadn't run up against any Reb pickets. He prayed that he could find Shields's corpse. The way was clear enough. He should almost be there.

WITH THIS RING

A half moon shone down through an opening in the clouds. The ground lay littered with man-sized mounds partly obscured by the fog. The cold night kept the stench down, but the corpses had festered during the day, so a sickly sweet rancor was present. A faint glint off one corpse gave Bowles pause. Around the neck of Jessup's corpse he saw the gold chain and Minie ball. A slug had took out the back of Jessup's head. Guess his road had ended afore Richmond. He searched the pockets and stuffed what he'd found in his own to mail off to Jessup's kin. Maybe this kindness could help erase the guilt of what he'd done this day.

Most like just another fool's errand.

Bowles squatted in the middle of a familiar looking clearing. Shields lay just over this rise. Of that he was sure, but the tightness in his gut and the pounding of his heart kept him rooted to this spot till the *clank* of metal close by forced his hand.

Shields's face was briefly lit in the light then the moon passed behind some clouds. But it hadn't passed quick enough to miss the look of surprise that was still painted across his face. Bowles tried to close Shields's eyes but something stopped his fingers from doing so —maybe that same hand of Providence that helped him to find this spot.

In his right hand Shields clutched the sealed envelope. Bowles pried the fingers open, removing it with shaking hands.

He opened the bloodstained letter, but it was too dark to read and too dangerous to spark a fire. The moon passed into view again and he made out some of Sarah's words:

"Dearest Robert," it read. "It is you I love. As for James, you have done him a grave disservice. I pray you come to this realization before reading these lines..."

The moonlight faded once more. Further uphill came the sounds of approaching graybacks.

As the sounds of southern voices grew near, he removed Shields's haversack, took Sarah's ring and worked it onto Shields's wedding finger.

He felt nothing, as though he'd been emptied of all goodness. But there was heaps of fighting ahead, and heaps of charges to lead till he paid in full measure for what he'd done this day.

Clouds covered the moon and he was left in darkness. He turned back toward the Federal lines.

"Well, *Sergeant*," he said under his breath. "Best be gettin' off this damned hill."

TWISTED BUT NEVER BROKEN

ROB VAGLE

Rob Vagle writes one of my favorite recurring characters, Guillermo Tavarez. Guillermo takes action that some of us think about, but wouldn't be capable of actually doing. Two more Guillermo Tavarez stories appear in Rob's collection, The Devil Is in the Dust. *Yet another appeared in our* Holiday Spectacular *in 2020, and will be part of the ebook release of the* Holiday Spectacular #2. *To find out more about Guillermo and Rob's other work, go to robvagle.com.*

Guillermo's lungs burned and he stopped underneath the carport and relished the feel of the blood pulsing through his veins, pumping through his muscles, and his heart hammering in his chest.

Sweat trickled down his neck and soaked his A-shirt. The sun was low in the west and the sky was a gash of red and pink. The weather had broken, merciful. The summer monsoon season in Phoenix had retreated, the humidity discarded, and the cool evening air invigorated Guillermo.

October brought cooler evenings. A month ago he would have preferred to go into his trailer with the swamp cooler and out of the heat, but tonight with the sweat pouring down his face and neck, he preferred to catch his breath outside after his run and stand in the low light of the dying day.

With the sun low in the sky, the mesquite's shadow stretched to the edge of the carport. The mesquite tree stood tall with two limbs that had crossed over one another a long time ago. Then, sometime later, the limbs crossed back over one another again, creating a twisted look like two flexible human fingers that managed to do a double cross. Guillermo wondered how the tree could survive in this twisted way. The mesquite was far from broken or dying. Off shoots of smaller limbs and branches twisted among one another, some curling back to launch back up through the upper canopy of the tree. The leaves were narrow, long, and feathery. Green all year long. And the thick thorns on the branches could either be used as toothpicks or pierce human flesh.

The mesquite was on his cousin's property. They lived on the south side of Phoenix where more subdivisions were being built but they were still out of reach of the developement for at least a mile. Out here, there wasn't much except for rock and dust, and a landscape dotted with palm trees. Some palm trees still had their skirts and in the evening light they looked like angels with their wings tight against their backs as if they were cowering at the incessant approach of night.

His own little space on his cousin's property included the one-bedroom trailer with a carport with ample space for his Mustang, barbells, workout bench, and heavy bag. Inside the trailer, he also had his office, but he never met his clients here on the property on the southern outskirts of the city. As a private detective or a fixer (a fijador), he went out to meet his clients. Someday soon, Guillermo hoped he could get an office closer to downtown so that he could offer his services to lawyers and insurance agents.

Maria, his cousin, and her family lived in the eight-room ranch style home. She worked as a professor of Latin American studies at Arizona State University and her husband, Marco, was a successful businessman with a car repair business with six locations scattered in the east and west valleys.

At the front of the house the landscape was more cultivated with cactus and agave. In the back where Guillermo's trailer was, some palm trees, and the twisted mesquite.

"Hey, Guillermo."

He pivoted on his feet, raising dust over his shoes. He looked downward to find Jose's friend, Reikan, eyes wide, hands up, and he took a step backwards. He hadn't heard the boy approach from the back of the house.

"Whoa, I didn't think it was possible to scare you."

Reikan wore blue jeans and dark blue shirt with a Captain America shield on the front of it. He'd been coming home with Jose after school for the past three days, and yesterday he even stayed for dinner. They watched movies, played Nintendo, or played soccer in the dusty yard underneath the Khadrawy Palm Trees (Reikan knew palm trees from visiting Iraq where his father and mother were born).

Like Guillermo, Reikan was first-generation American born. Reikan had long bangs, tall and skinny with long limbs. He was the second youngest—at twelve—sibling in a family of three boys and five girls.

"You got some good sneak," Guillermo said.

He gave the boy a smile, fully aware there had been a wild look in his eye when the boy surprised him. Guillermo wasn't enamored with that part of himself. If he was religious like his mother, he'd call it the devil, but he didn't believe in a god or devil. There was only humanity, which contained extremes, from the love and generosity of a college professor leaving water for illegals crossing the U.S. Mexican border to the darker and violent gringos that shoot—for sport—illegals crossing the border.

The dark part of himself surfaced when needed and served him well. He had found little atonement. The respites helped, like when he had been alone in the dying light of day contemplating the twisted growth of a mesquite tree. He helped others with generosity and service, finding justice within the light and dark extremes of humanity.

Reikan returned the smile and Guillermo felt relieved. The air smelled earthy and sweet, the smell of the mesquite tree. He felt relaxed after his run, like water ready to pool on the ground. But he wasn't ready to be done. Physical exertion was another thing—paradoxically—that calmed him. He still had some heavy-bag work to do underneath the carport, behind the back bumper of his Mustang.

Then Reikan's smile slipped away like the sun and he rubbed at his left arm. "I wanted to talk to you, is all."

"Go for it."

"My sister is missing. I have a bad feeling about it."

The boy couldn't stop staring at the tattoos running up Guillermo's exposed arms and neck.

"What's the bad feeling?" he asked.

"My father didn't like how Nadia was acting. Always complaining she was wearing tight jeans and stuff like that. He didn't like the way she took selfies with boys. To me they just had their arms around each other when I saw them, but my father called it hugging."

"What about the bad feeling, Reikan?"

The boy looked down at his feet as he scraped at the dirt. "It's complicated."

"Has your father called the police?"

He nodded and continued to rub at his left arm.

"How old is Nadia?"

"Eighteen."

"She live outside the house?"

"Yes. That's the problem. My father thinks she should stay with the family. Only leave when she's married to someone. There was such a man when we visited Iraq. Nadia didn't want anything to do with him."

"They don't sound like they're on good terms, your sister and father. Nadia's is keeping her distance."

Reikan shook his head side to side like an animal snapping the neck of a small animal.

"No," he said. "He warned her. He told her if she didn't come around there would be consequences."

Guillermo felt a cold stone drop into his stomach. Now he had a bad feeling about this. Some people came to this country with the ways from their former one. The old ways were too powerful to give up, no matter what the cost.

"All the more reason to stay away," Guillermo said, hoping that was all there was to it.

"Nobody has seen her. Not her friends. Nobody." Reikan pulled his phone out of his front pocket. "I'll show you something else."

Reikan carried an old Nokia phone, even small in the boy's hands. He pressed some of the buttons on the face as he said, "I saw this man outside when I went to school this morning. He sits in a pickup truck with peeling paint on the hood. He asked if I've seen my sister, Nadia. When I said no, he said to 'tell my father people would like to know where she is.' He said, 'Tell him it's a matter of little time before they know. Soon, my little Muslim,' he called me, 'tell him soon.'"

Reikan then held out his phone for him. "I took his picture. He thought I'd show it to my father, but my father already knows this man has been around."

Guillermo took the phone and said, "Your father knows this man?"

"I think so. He makes my father very angry."

When Guillermo raised the phone to his face he recognized the Caucasian man with the gray beard. A bad feeling tightened around his spine. It was not a good thing that Reikan's father knew this man or his services.

Guillermo, however, held his facial expression as hard as stone not to give anything away.

He gave the phone back to Reikan who looked up at him with all the hope of a meek little dog in the pound. As if the picture meant everything. It meant there was proof something bad had happened to Nadia.

Damnit to hell, the kid was right.

Guillermo's heartbeat had slowed from his run. His mouth was dry, his body in need of water.

"Would you like something to drink?" he asked Reikan. "I'm parched. We can talk more about your sister after I get us drinks."

"No thank you, I'm not thirsty," he said.

"Come sit with me while I have some agua."

With a glance at the back of the house, Reikan followed.

The gray bearded white man in the picture was Jesus, pronounced in the Spanish form, "hay-soos."

Jesus dealt with the dead. He hid the bodies of the murdered. Bodies hidden to hobble any form of justice. He'd make a body vanish for anyone.

The carport was wide enough for two cars, but Guillermo only had the Mustang. The extended carport, however, reached over the front stoop and provided shade. He pointed Reikan to the two green plastic chairs next to the steps. Guillermo's bottle of water was sitting on the upside down milk crate between the chairs. When he sat down he grabbed the bottle, opened it, and drank deeply as he watched Reikan. The boy had stopped rubbing his arm, but he still fidgeted. This time his feet, his red Converse shoes, scraped back and forth on the gravel in the driveway.

The water hit Guillermo's tongue and seemed to fill every pore there. The water sharpened his focus and as often was the case, it worked like caffeine. It perked him up.

Guillermo had heard of families coming from more conservative countries like Iraq and their head-on collision with Western culture. In America where there were more freedoms (but even then there were limits, and that also varied depending on who you were and where you were from) caused a great deal of culture shock.

The culture of the old world often doesn't survive in the same form in the new world.

Reikan believed his father killed his sister for the family's honor, yet Reikan was too scared or ashamed to admit it.

"Do you really believe your father killed your sister?"

"I said she was missing." The boy had a good mask on his face. He looked like he believed it, but his eyes were glossy and he blinked. Repeatedly.

"You also said you had a bad feeling. You haven't elaborated on the matter."

"My brother said they took care of their girls in Iraq. He didn't mean it in a good way."

"You mean in a loving way, Reikan?"

"No. No, there's no love involved in it. They do it to preserve the family's honor. But we're not in Iraq anymore. When I brought this up to Jamil—that's my brother, he's the oldest—he told me I was blind because of the Westerners. He told me I never lived in Iraq and I was already lost."

"What did you think about Nadia's refusal to conform to your father's wishes?"

"She wanted what she wanted."

"Which was?"

"She wanted to go to college and study psychology or maybe journalism. She liked the aerial classes she was taking, she was learning to perform on silks and trapeze. She would be expected to bear children and cook and clean if she got married. That wasn't Nadia."

"What about your mother in all this?"

"She tells my father Nadia is a lost cause. That she's a terrible influence on her sisters."

"Reikan, are you afraid your father killed Nadia?"

The boy's mask broke at that question. Tears welled up in his eyes and ran down his cheeks. He shuddered and a cry escaped his mouth. Reikan couldn't speak and all he could do was shake his head.

Guillermo's heart broke for the boy, but he didn't regret asking the question. He felt there was a real danger here, and Nadia, perhaps, was already lost.

The news of Nadia's death would hurt Reikan more. The boy had to know that bad news was on the horizon. How could he go about his day without hope of ever seeing his sister again, knowing something bad had happened to her, but not receiving any truth, and knowing his father had a hand in it. No proof might be easier on his heart, but it certainly wouldn't be justice for Nadia.

Reikan's voice broke as he said, "I don't want it to be true."

Then he had no more control as another cry bubbled from deep in his throat and he covered his face with his hands.

The next morning, Guillermo drove his '77 Mustang to Reikan's home. The Khalafs lived in the south end of Scottsdale in a split-level home with a two car garage, clay-tiled roof, granite beds with agave and Palo Verde trees.

Guillermo didn't see a pickup truck with peeling paint out front so he drove on by, with a glance at the house which was quiet. There was a blue Ford Explorer parked in the driveway.

Guillermo last saw Jesus in a little hole in the wall bar on Broadway Road near Skyharbor. That was where the man could be found if one needed a body to be disposed of. Guillermo had been on a case locating a missing white man with a connection to drug dealers when he was directed to Jesus. Guillermo didn't much care for the man's choice of business and his lack of concern of the activities that brought people to his door. Jesus never asked questions about the "package" he was making vanish. He needed some requirements like the body wrapped in plastic and delivered to an agreed upon location.

The bar was called Pair Of Dice, a cinderblock building with a gravel parking lot. When the Mustang's tires crunched over gravel there was only one vehicle in the parking lot before noon on a weekday. It was a white GMC pickup with peeling paint on the hood.

Guillermo parked next to it and when he got out of the Mustang, he could hear Guns & Roses playing inside the bar. It wasn't loud. It was just that the door was open. The inside smelled like cigarettes and stale beer.

He walked over the threshold into a dim lighted bar with a dusty white linoleum floor. The Guns & Roses was being piped in through speakers in the corner, the sound turned down the moment he entered. Ceiling fans circulated the air in the room, but it didn't make the room any fresher. The room was stuffy, but bearable. By mid-afternoon it would be unbearable if the door stayed open. The bar ran along the wall to Guillermo's left and Jesus sat at the end of the bar with his body faced toward the door.

He had a cocktail glass in front of him which looked like it contained orange juice. He had a newspaper open in front of him and when Guillermo walked in Jesus had his hand on the gun holstered at his hip.

It had been at least six months since Guillermo had last talked to Jesus, yet the man remembered him instantly.

"Hola, Guillermo, cómo estás?" Jesus said, removing his hand from the gun. "Anybody tell you you're too handsome for a shithole like this?"

The place was empty. The half dozen round tables had been wiped off with their chairs tucked neatly underneath. The bar was blond wood with initials and symbols carved into it over the decades.

Guillermo sat on the stool next to Jesus. The upholstered backrest had a gash in the back, its yellow stuffing exposed.

"Can I offer you a mimosa?" Jesus asked.

"No thank you," Guillermo said, and got right to the point. "Seriously, Jesus, getting into blackmail now?"

Jesus gave him a double take and shook his head. "Here I thought you might be bringing me business, not getting your nose up in my shit. Again."

"You've been lurking outside the Khalaf's home. You only deal with the dead. Unless maybe there's a problem with negotiating with the living," Guillermo said.

Jesus's eyes lit up at the name Khalaf and he grinned. "Who would come talk to you?"

"Maybe it was their daughter Nadia."

Jesus snorted and waved a hand. "The police aren't even looking for her. They're more interested in her father."

That was something Reikan hadn't mentioned. Guillermo wondered if the boy even knew the police were talking to his father.

Jesus continued. "You got me bent over a barrel. I don't know where you're coming from. You wouldn't be working for the police."

"Why wouldn't I?"

"I've known many types of men. You're too dark, Guillermo. Too dark to be working for the police. Khalaf is too deep in the hole to pay someone like you to shake me up or get rid of me. You came strolling in here without a gun at your side. I don't think you mean me harm. You want to get up in my shit, yes, but you're not here to break kneecaps."

Jesus removed his hand from the top of the bar to the gun on his hip. "Or am I wrong?"

"I'm not working for Khalaf. I'm doing a family member a favor.

They don't know where Nadia is and they don't think Mr. Khalaf is going to win father of the year."

Jesus raised his hand from his gun, gave Guillermo a thumbs up, and picked up his mimosa and drank some. After he smacked his lips, he said, "Thank you for being straight with me. You don't, I'll shut you out. I don't know how much I can help you. I need the rest of the money from Khalaf."

"I need to know where Nadia is."

Jesus snorted again. "I don't know her from Adam. All I know is I took care of a package from Khalaf."

"Where did you put that package?"

"You know that's not on the table."

"How does somebody like you get stiffed on payment. Seems like you should have better business practices than that."

"Hey, it happens to the best of us." Jesus considered Guillermo and leaned in close and said, "How was I to know that Khalaf's oldest son, Marwan, would bring me the package with only half the money. I was expecting Khalaf and I got Marwan. Apparently his son is the one with the gambling problem. Marwan says he stopped off at Talking Stick to gain some dinero off his father's money. Claims he had lost half of it. The boy is—what?—in his twenties, past drinking age and he's crying like a baby. Don't tell my father. I'll pay you, I'll pay you, just be patient." Jesus threw up his hands in mock surrender.

"You have a soft spot, Jesus?"

Jesus ignored him. "Marwan practically vanishes. What do I find when I start following Khalaf? He's the one hitting the casinos. So yes, I took a boy at his word, my mistake. That's no goddamn soft spot. Khalaf has to pay."

"Or you'll tell the police where Nadia is."

"Damn straight. That's my angle. I'd rather receive the money."

"How did you know the police have been talking to him?"

"I've seen police at his door and it wasn't because I spoke to them, so don't make those kind of assumptions, Guillermo."

"I wasn't. I want to know how you know."

"The man was stalking his own daughter. He knew where she worked and both he and his wife would show up and make asses of themselves pleading for Nadia to think about the family and how it would look if their daughter was out running free."

"Were you there, Jesus? Sounds like you really got to know the whole family."

"I heard all that from your client," Jesus said. "I know exactly who talked to you."

Guillermo sat back. He didn't think Reikan had told these things to Jesus. Their conversation described by Reikan revolved around Jesus's picture.

Jesus rolled his eyes. "Nadia's sister told me these things. You're not the only gumshoe, amigo. I have my ways, too, at finding information."

Guillermo felt a deep sense of relief Nadia's siblings were looking for her, being aware of her, and helping out when they could. He wondered if Reikan was so distraught, not only because of what may have happened to his sister, but what might happen to him and the rest of the family. Living under the Khalaf room sounded like hell, stifling, with Khalaf controlling, maybe violent, even as his eighteen-year-old daughter fled from home.

"That's why the police are pressing him so hard about their missing daughter. He's already a suspect because of the scenes he caused. Nadia got help from the police when she moved out of the house, you know that? They were there in case her old man got out of hand. Khalaf is a rat in a cage right now."

"Now that you're no longer lurking outside their house, I assume Khalaf got your message?" Guillermo said.

"He did. If he doesn't get me the money by the end of today, I'll notify the police where to find Nadia. The Iraqui son of a bitch is going to cost me a dumping ground."

Guillermo slid off the stool. "Thank you for your time," he said.

"Gracias for stopping by," Jesus said. "Don't do anything stupid now that might prevent me from getting my money."

Sweat trickled down the back of Guillermo's neck. It had gotten stuffier inside Pair Of Dice. He ignored Jesus and walked for the door. The sunbeam on the dusty linoleum floor from the open doorway was bright enough to make him squint.

Jesus called, "Amigo, did I ever tell you I'm half Hispanic? My mother was from El Salvador, but my papa was here in America. I don't usually claim my Hispanic heritage but there you have it. Yeah, I know, the name Jesus is just giving it away."

Guillermo stopped inside the doorway with the sun on half his face as he turned back to Jesus. The man still sat at the stool with one hand on the bar and his other arm propped up at the elbow on the chair back. Guillermo shrugged.

"You can trust me, amigo," Jesus said. "Maybe you have your ways of taking care of packages, that's fine. Keep me in mind if you're in a pinch. I'll give you a deal."

Guillermo hated the way Jesus looked at him, as if he knew him. He felt his spine tighten like someone had ratcheted up the tension.

"I don't have any packages," Guillermo said.

Jesus snorted. "Play it that way. If you haven't by now, you will someday. All I'm saying is keep my service in mind."

With that, Jesus turned back to the bar with his newspaper and mimosa.

When Guillermo slipped behind the wheel of his Mustang, the confirmation that Nadia had been murdered stirred up his insides. He couldn't help thinking of a dust devil whirling up inside of him. Nadia had died at the hands of her father who did everything to erase the young woman.

That didn't sit well with Guillermo. Not with the fact there were more daughters at Khalaf's home, let alone Reikan who grew up here in the United States and who didn't understand, or at least questioned, the old ways of the country and society Khalaf had come from.

As Guillermo left the parking lot of Pair Of Dice, he couldn't convince himself Khalaf's home was the place to go. With the air conditioning blasting cool air on his arms, he turned the Mustang west on Broadway.

Broadway Road had numerous office parks, a pawn shop, a Seven Eleven, and a gas station. The office park he pulled into looked like it had been abandoned. There were two cars parked outside the Adobe-like building, probably built in the seventies. It was single level with walkways leading inside the complex. He caught sight of a green courtyard within the center of the complex at the end of those walkways as he drove by. He parked his Mustang in a space facing the street underneath a large Afghan Pine. He had an easy view of Pair Of Dice.

And he waited.

He had seen the indicators from Jesus. The man had the door open, he seemed aware of who was coming in the parking lot, and he had his gun. He was expecting Khalaf and he was prepared for trouble if it should present itself.

The more Guillermo thought about it, the more sense it made for Khalaf to remove Jesus from the picture. Before Jesus informed the police where to find Nadia.

It was more likely Khalaf would go that route. Khalaf could somehow obtain the money needed. Which pointed to a Pair Of Dice once again.

It was times like these Guillermo knew the benefit of having a partner. The partner could stake out Khalaf's home, because Khalaf could as likely flee the city.

Guillermo did not want a partner. This was his own work. His private work.

Guillermo sat there for two hours before his stomach growling became unbearable. It was way past a break and he was contemplating driving to the gas station for something to eat when a blue Ford Explorer—the very same one he had seen in Khalaf's driveway earlier in the day—pulled into the Pair Of Dice parking lot and parked next to Jesus's truck. It had been the only vehicle to pull in there for the last two hours. The only visitor into the bar had been from a long-haired shirtless man pushing a shopping cart full of cans and bottles. He came out with a full garbage bag that he piled on top of the rest of his hoard in the cart.

He observed two men get out of the Explorer. One, the driver, was a middle-aged man with a paunch dressed in a Polo shirt and black slacks. The passenger was younger, tall and thin. Wearing a white shirt, light dark jacket, and black slacks.

Guillermo wasn't interested in Jesus's safety. The man had been prepared if the situation should go south.

One of two things would go down upon the two men entering Pair Of Dice. Either they brought the money and there would be no violence. If Khafla and his son tried to rough Jesus up in any way, certain violence would be unleashed.

Guillermo leaned over, opened the glove box and pulled out his Beretta. He placed it in the empty passenger seat.

He waited until the two men went through the open doorway. The son stopped and looked inside as if listening to someone, then he abandoned the door and entered.

Guillermo started up the Mustang and backed out. Traffic was heavy on Broadway and he had to wait for what seemed like a minute to exit the office park, and then another thirty seconds for a break in westbound traffic before he could turn into the Pair Of Dice lot. He let the Mustang roll across the gravel, steering the hood toward the open front door of the bar.

His pulse increased and he could feel it pounding through his neck. He could hear the blood flowing in his ears.

The son stepped into the doorway with one hand in the pocket of his light jacket. His face slacked at the sight of the Mustang's grill heading for the front door.

Guillermo stepped on the brake and the tires slid on the gravel. The Mustang stopped two feet from the building. The son, eyes wide and in a state of panic, pulled at the door.

Guillermo grabbed the Beretta and slipped out of the car. The son had managed to pull the door toward him. Guillermo grabbed the edge of the door and threw it open again. He then forced his way inside.

The son pulled a chair from a nearby table, its legs squawking across the linoleum, to put between him and Guillermo. When the son's hand came out of his jacket with a handgun, Guillermo kicked the chair sliding into his midsection. The son buckled at the waist and the gun in his hand pointed downward.

Over the son's shoulder, at the bar, Jesus, behind the bar had his own gun in his hand which was raised with barrel pointed at the ceiling. His other hand was on Khalaf's shoulder. Both stood on the customer side of the bar.

Guillermo ripped the gun from the son's hand and raised his right knee high and kicked the young man in the solar plexus. He fell onto the table and off the other side. The table cracked when it hit the floor and chairs tumbled to the floor.

"I told you not to do anything stupid, muchacho," Jesus said.

He now had his gun leveled at Guillermo. Khalaf charged, which surprised Guillermo. Khalaf was a large man and had the gait of a grizzly bear. Guillermo raised the Beretta but Khalaf had an expandable baton. The tip flew at Guillermo's face. He whipped his head back to avoid being struck and lashed out with the hand holding the son's gun.

He connected with the side of Khalaf's face. Khalaf grimaced and his face turned beet red. Khalaf swung the expanded baton and struck Guillermo's shoulder, the pain so excruciating it felt like the baton had sunk into the muscle. Guillermo shoved the muzzle of the Beretta into Khalaf's paunch and pulled the trigger.

The gunshot cracked inside the small bar. The baton clattered to the floor and Khalaf crumpled after it, falling onto his side as blood oozed out of the wound, spreading across the linoleum.

"Pendajo," Jesus said. He stepped over the son and rushed to the door. With one quick glance outside, he pulled the door closed and locked the deadbolt.

Guillermo lowered himself to the floor, closer to the dying Khalaf. He had both hands over the wound and they were both covered in blood. His eyes were wild, seeing Guillermo over him, yet not acknowledging. He spoke rapidly, speaking in Arabic.

"For Nadia," Guillermo said.

Khalaf stopped speaking and his wild eyes suddenly settled on Guillermo.

"It's a mercy to rid you from this earth," Guillermo said.

A gunshot cracked inside bar and Guillermo was standing again. He raised his gun, then lowered it again when he saw what Jesus had done.

He had shot Khalaf's son. The remorse for the son covered Guillermo thick and heavy. Guillermo's rage had been aimed at Khalaf himself.

"The son didn't have to die," Guillermo said.

"No," Jesus said, "You signed his death warrant the moment you killed Khalaf with him in here. You know, this isn't what I had planned for my evening. You owe me and you can start by helping me clean up this mess."

It was two months before Guillermo saw Reikan again.

Guillermo had his head under the hood of the Mustang when the boy approached. It was just after four in the afternoon and the air was so cool it chilled Guillermo's skin. This time the boy made noises in the dirt as he walked up to the side of the car.

"Hey," Reikan said.

In the two months since he last spoke to Reikan, Nadia's body was recovered. Then, a month later, Khalaf's and his son's bodies were also recovered.

"Sorry about your sister," Guillermo said. "How's the rest of the family doing?"

"We miss Nadia," Reikan said.

Guillermo wiped his hands off on a shop rag and stood on the side of the car with Reikan. The two of them rested their backs against the car.

Guillermo pointed at the twisted mesquite tree and said, "There are forces that twist us. They threaten to break us, but we live on. Listen to your heart. Your sisters deserve to grow, Reikan. You were right to be concerned. Now they may grow, like you, without any twisting from your father."

In silence, they stood there for a long time.

WHAT BREAKS A MAN

KARI KILGORE

Kari Kilgore's stories usually have a bit of light and warmth. She writes about cats for our Year of the Cat series. She writes lovely holiday stories for our Holiday Spectacular. *But she has a dark side as well—her first novel was shortlisted for a Stoker award—one you can discover more about at* karikilgore.com

Her inspiration for this story came from a strange moment in her life. She writes, "What Breaks a Man got its spark on a drive from Virginia to Austin, Texas. While basically parked in awful traffic on the broiling hot interstate, I noticed supports for a missing bridge looming overhead. The thick rebar twisted in different directions and was coated in rust, so I wondered whether the bridge was never finished or had been removed. I eventually took a random exit that looked abandoned, trusting my GPS's promise to get me around the mess. It did, but I always wondered how that might have gone for a different person, on a darker trip."

Reggie gripped the bottom of the hot, sticky steering wheel, focusing on the ache in his scarred and swollen knuckles. The snarled construction traffic inched forward just often enough that he couldn't put the car into park and stretch his cramped right foot. The oily stink of exhaust floated through the open windows to compete with the reek of weed and cigarettes ground into the stained, faded cloth seats. Motionless, humid air did nothing to clear out the sweetish aroma of gas from the hatchback.

Now that he was stuck in it, Reggie felt guilty about making his kid drive this heap even after the air conditioner quit working.

The decaying, grubby black padding was missing along the top of the steering wheel, and the dark exposed metal was too hot to touch after baking in the July Texas sun for days. Reggie had yelled when his son picked the rotten foam off when he was sixteen, wondering why he was so stupid even with a fifteen-year-old beater of a car.

Scotty had answered with a shrug, as usual, before slamming his bedroom door. That surly kid hadn't stopped trying to escape his screwed-up family since the day he was born. Not much different than Reggie, really.

Except Scotty may have finally managed the trick this time.

Reggie leaned forward and pulled his wet T-shirt away from his back even though it was useless with the sweat-soaked seat. The oil-stained work cooler in the filthy passenger floorboard only had a couple of cheap beers floating in more water than ice. He could still taste the bitter remains of the last one in the back of his throat, and the flavor wouldn't be any better lukewarm.

That didn't mean he wasn't going to pop one of the disgusting things open to wash down a couple of Percocets before this blasted traffic broke up.

The eighteen-wheeler on his left ground its gears loud enough that Reggie flinched away, then it jounced forward before the air brakes hissed. The interstate ran though a concrete gully of half-built overpasses, perpetually delayed by some corrupt politician or other, concentrating the fumes and dust into a toxic haze.

Even with dozens of Texas license plates between pulsing brake lights caging him in, no one was taking the exit just ahead. The steep ramp looked abandoned somehow, with weeds growing in the cracks in the pavement and drifts of garbage along both sides. Stubby, broken pillars of concrete fringed with twisted exposed metal rebar jutted out from the walls above the highway, all that remained of a strangely absent bridge.

Voices whispered up out of Reggie's brain, crawling down his neck and twisting his already tight shoulders. Take your work GPS, his buddies down at the garage said. The boss won't know. Don't want to get lost down there in the ass-end of nowhere Texas. Just throw it in your suitcase. Don't be an idiot.

If you're going on this fool trip, they said, at least ditch your damn stubborn pride and get a smart phone.

Ignoring the latest dig about dropping a fortune on a pocket computer when he didn't even own a flip phone was easy enough. So was leaving the chattery electronic travel brain safely at home, tossed in the floorboard of Reggie's latest dealership employee special. Much as it got on his nerves when it demanded he take a U-turn or recalculated for what felt like hours, the thing would have given him a way out of this snarled traffic.

Maybe even that exit, the one no one had ventured onto while cars and trucks inched and braked, inched and braked.

The idea of his expensive work-trip nanny sitting on this cracked and faded dashboard felt obscene, anyway. The gadget was probably worth more than the whole car.

The only link to the outside world was one Reggie hadn't paid or planned for. A small grey pager, so ancient he thought it might have been a derelict from the 90s, tucked in the glove box along with a drift of old registrations and solidified ketchup packets. The thing fit in his palm. Nothing but a tiny one-line screen on the end, a built-in belt clip, and a couple of shredded rubber buttons, like someone was in the habit of digging at them with a key.

It powered on, but he had no idea whether it was activated or what the phone number could be. Everything that might have identified it had been scratched off, maybe by that same key. Reggie had slipped it into his pocket, still not sure why.

Another voice, one Reggie was more likely to scream at than listen to even after thirty years, whispered through his mind. *Why are you driving this rolling death trap, then? Drop it off at the closest junkyard and let the crusher do its work. Better yet, park the nasty thing right here and walk away. They'll either tow it away or let it rot and crumble in the sun.*

Then his own voice.

You know how to walk away, Reggie.

Instead of letting that settle into the space between his ears, Reggie jerked the steering wheel to his right, getting a shuddering response from the leaky power steering pump for his trouble. His right foot ached to stomp on the gas pedal, if nothing else to get a fresh breeze through the windows. Dealing with a stalled engine on top of everything else might force him to discover what he did when a day like this finally broke him, so he eased forward instead.

The gap he'd left in the endless line of vehicles closed before he got all four wheels onto the ramp, a gleaming orange Hummer jumping ahead in a heartbeat.

Decision made, then. Get on with it.

For what had to be the hundredth time in the seven or eight miles he'd managed of a thousand mile trip, he wished the heap had a manual transmission. The creaky old automatic whined higher and higher on the sharp grade of the off-ramp, but it refused to change gears.

Maybe with a stick, Reggie could downshift, hit the gas, and launch this whole disaster over the other side of the ramp. Crashing on top of some perfectly maintained suburban SUV, breaching the fine-tuned climate control and yanking the overly pampered driver out of cell phone oblivion, would be worth a couple of scrapes and bruises.

Reggie shook his head and craned his grubby, aching neck, trying to get the lay of whatever land he'd just rolled himself into at a blazing fourteen miles an hour.

The desolation and decay of the highway didn't improve with the change in elevation. A row of low concrete barricades, shoved out of line and piled up with garbage, made a halfhearted attempt to stop cars from driving out into nothing. Reggie wondered how long ago the highway department forgot this place ever existed.

That temptation surged in him again, the desire to see how many of the blocks he could ram over the edge before the junker died.

Or before someone stopped him.

The ramp he'd expected, and halfway planned to follow back onto the highway, was blocked by more of the same crumbling barricades. Unless he was willing to take his chances and reverse back down into the nightmare traffic jam, turning right was the only option. The road was nothing but old concrete slabs, faded to nearly white and full of cracks. It cut straight through a vast industrial wasteland full of rusting shell buildings and empty parking lots before curving off to the right.

No other vehicles up here, though, clogging up the freeway and the air. Even better, no people.

Reggie didn't have much choice, but he still felt a tiny thrill of satisfaction when he turned and kept going.

He realized his mistake after less than five minutes of following slow curves through acres of wasted factories and dead grass. Without the crush of cars and people to keep him angry and distracted, his thoughts kept veering back to the same sickening topic like the car trying to drag itself to the left.

The dealership's chirpy receptionist over the echoing garage intercom, telling everyone within earshot that there was a call for Reggie Cox. Straightening from the boss's late Sixties Camaro, wiping his hands to keep from smudging up the office phone.

That voice on the other end, clear enough to hear how hard Scotty had been breathing, even though the kid was whispering.

Trouble.

Some kind of trouble, big enough that Scotty would be disappearing for a while. Probably a long while.

Reggie too shocked with a phone call after years of silence to insist on knowing, understanding, before the kid hung up.

Maybe asking if he could help.

He slowed the junker, the one he'd made his son drive to supposedly force him to learn to work on them like the old man. Grabbed one of the warm beers. Swallowed half of it with the Percocet.

Before that day had ended, Reggie had somehow booked a one-way flight to Texas. He didn't remember making the call, but the charge to his credit card showed up along with the ticket in his work email the next day.

Stupid, that. Not having a computer or smart phone meant he only used email that didn't even pretend to be private.

A smart phone might have shown him the number Scotty called from, too.

He did remember cracking into more than beer once he got home. He'd found the empty bottle of Wild Turkey in the trash the next morning, staggering around the kitchen wondering what smashed his head with a baseball bat overnight. That explained the plane ticket.

His least favorite voice piped up in his head, as usual when Reggie'd done something even though he should have known better.

You didn't have to get on that plane, son. You could have reported that credit card stolen, shut the whole thing off. Or just eaten the cost and not made this whole mess worse by throwing yourself into the middle of it.

"Thanks, Mom," he said, not surprised by the rough edge to his voice. "Always knew how to make it all worse in the end."

Reggie forced his attention back to the road, hitting the brakes hard enough that the heap skidded sideways. A row of modern black and yellow barricades stretched across, blocking what looked like another several miles of abandoned industrial wasteland.

Why the hell hadn't someone done that on both sides, or blocked the highway exit?

A well-maintained road cut across his path, fresh black pavement and bright white lines as far as he could see in both directions. Still no houses or any other kind of buildings, but this had to be better than driving deeper into nothing at all. His tour of dead American manufacturing jobs wouldn't get him any closer to Ohio before he had to be back at work or lose his own job.

He considered for a second, looking at the sinking sun to find west, tapping his chewed fingernails on his leg. He'd probably hit some kind of civilization faster if he turned right again, toward the medium-sized city he'd come from. Where Scotty had been living. But he'd be going south, making a longer drive for himself in the end.

The nearly full gas tank, typical for an old car you checked the oil in before the gas, made his choice for him. North it was.

Reggie's mood even brightened for a minute. A cool breeze blew his hair back as the car finally topped forty miles an hour, and the Percocet was starting to kick in. If only he had a stack of old cassette tapes on the seat beside him, he could be the guy in his early twenties on a road trip.

His whole life ahead of him, as vast and endless as the arteries and veins of asphalt across the continent.

But Scotty was the one in his twenties, not creeping up on fifty like Reggie. And just like Reggie, he'd closed off one of those paths after another, barricades made of anger and rock-solid grudges instead of concrete putting him on the same predictable path.

Scotty hadn't knocked up his high school girlfriend and given up on college, then never let that girlfriend forget it. But he had run off before he even finished high school, then gotten himself caught up in something terrible down here. Something so bad he hadn't even thrown it in Reggie's face to point out what a failure he'd been as a father.

When the pager buzzed against his leg, Reggie jumped so hard he jerked the steering wheel. Only the sluggish power steering kept him from driving straight into the concrete drainage ditch that was his only companion through dusty farmland all around. He fumbled the thing out, hoping he could manage to activate the ancient screen.

Digging his fingertip into one of the shredded buttons rewarded him with a phone number he didn't recognize followed by 911. Old pager talk for call right now unless things had changed. Call right now, with no cell phone and the odds of finding a pay phone slim to none no matter where he was. The area code was strange too, like one of the new ones for an overcrowded city, or only for cell phones.

None of that mattered unless he could find a phone, any phone. Reggie put the pager carefully on the passenger seat, afraid of draining what had to be a primitive battery. He nudged the car up to fifty-five, close enough to the last speed limit sign he'd seen.

His mind, his own voice instead of his mother's, protested that getting pulled over for speeding would be a perfect way to end this trip early. Depending on what Scotty had done, police might be looking for even this junk pile. Or that pager. They'd certainly be wondering who'd broken into Scotty's apartment, using the same credit card to defeat the cheap lock.

The place had been surprisingly neat, nothing like the room Scotty had tried his best to destroy at home. It barely looked lived in. Beige walls, tan furniture that would fit in at a doctor's office. The sign out front said apartments, but Reggie would have sworn he was in one of the extended-stay hotels the dealership put him up in when he had to travel for training.

Going on nothing but some kind of vague notion that he was helping Scotty, he'd gathered up the few things he was sure didn't belong there. The garbage bags in the kitchen and bathroom. The hatchback stank so strongly of gas that it covered up the faint rotting food smells of the garbage. A couple of shirts and socks that looked like they'd been dropped. A few books. Anything he thought someone could follow back to his son.

The key he'd had already, stashed away years ago in case Scotty locked himself out. He never had, at least not out of the car.

The road finally curved toward the left, back toward the highway, and Reggie spotted clusters of houses on both sides in the distance. When he got closer, several more sprouted up against the farmland. He barked harsh laughter when the tall blue and white sign of a gas station towered over everything else.

He got the heap parked in the lumpy parking lot, dug several quarters out of his pocket, and grabbed the pager. Maybe, just maybe this place was run down and faded enough to still have a pay phone lurking inside. The wrinkly cigarette ads covering the smudged windows had to be a good sign. If nothing else, maybe he could bribe the kid behind the counter to use the phone back there.

He found neither in the fog of stale smoke and overcooked coffee, but the scrawny girl agreed to let Reggie use her cell phone for the low fee of five dollars. Reggie wondered how much she'd pocketed with that little trick, but he handed the money over and walked to the other side of the store. The rows of glass-fronted beverage cases had seen better days, and they'd surely been cleaner. Reggie wanted any privacy he could get.

Someone picked up on the first ring.

Scotty.

"Who the hell is this?"

"It's your father, Scotty. What's going on?"

"You have my car or just the pager?"

Reggie took a deep breath, blowing out condensation on the glass.

"I have the car. I thought it would be better if no one could find it."

"I don't think the car's going to make much of a difference at this point."

"Scotty, what's happening? What can I do?"

"Are you on a cell phone?"

"Yeah," Reggie said. "Not mine, though."

"I didn't think it would be yours. But someone might trace it. I won't be here for long, so it won't—"

"Tell me where you are, or at least a phone number! Let me do something to help you."

"That's what I was trying to do. Got a pen or something?"

Reggie walked back up front and grabbed a pen and a piece of receipt from the register while the girl fiddled with the fountain soda machine.

"I'll be at this number in an hour," Scotty said. "How did you know where I live?"

"You're still on your mother's insurance, remember? She gave me the address. I didn't tell her why. You called me for some reason, son. Tell me what's going on."

Scotty sighed.

"I shouldn't have done that. We'd both be better off if you just went back home. Go buy a cheap cell phone, one without a contract. Call me in an hour. No promises."

A click, and he was gone.

Reggie stared up at the fluorescent lights overhead, one buzzing, one out. A scattering of dead bugs dotted the plastic covers. He blinked away tears before the girl could see them, thanked her, and left.

He sat in the car, face in his hands, trying not to shiver in the lingering heat. His damp shirt and the clammy fabric seat didn't help. Neither did the images tearing through his mind.

The last time he'd heard Scotty's voice was the day he'd left home a few months short of high school graduation. A last grand screaming match, and his son disappeared from his house and his life.

Scotty's mother left not long after. Reggie couldn't think of a single reason for her to stay, no matter how long and hard he tried. They both knew they'd only been staggering along in their marriage for years, hoping they could somehow make their son turn out okay.

Reggie had shown her part of what he'd found in Scotty's room when he pulled down a bunch of ratty old posters and a couple of framed photos.

The kid had punched holes in the drywall, evenly spaced and methodical. Like he was trying to beat the house until it gave up and fell down.

Reggie had never shown or even told anyone about the rest.

On the back of those posters, Scotty had scrawled on every inch of space. Some of it narrow and cramped, some sprawled and looping. Horrible filthy language and even worse ideas. About everything and everyone in his life. Especially his parents.

Reggie had read as much of it as he could decipher, unable to stop, knowing he'd remember the words and the fury and the imagined deeds for the rest of his own life. He'd crumpled the posters up and sat on his son's bed, sick and shaking, until his wife got home.

Exactly like he was sitting in the car Scotty had driven off in years ago.

A few miles down the road, he found a cell phone store and bought the only non-smart phone they had. No contract, free activation, a thousand minutes. The clerk told him about a cheap motel a little further on.

Reggie had time to check in, shower with harsh soap and scratchy towels, and call Scotty at exactly the promised time.

He had to look at the room phone to tell his son where he was.

"That town is a pit. Why the hell did you stop there?"

"So I could talk to you, Scotty."

The pause went on until Reggie was sure the call had dropped or he'd managed to turn the phone off.

"You're better off not knowing," Scotty finally said. "Go home. Tell yourself I'm somewhere doing just fine."

"I don't care about any of that. You're my son."

"Okay, you had your chance. I killed five people last week. Didn't plan to. Might have been a setup, to tell you the truth. But it's done."

Reggie closed his eyes, wondering if it was too late to stop now. Scotty's voice was calm and cold. He could have been talking about buying groceries or taking out the garbage.

"Bunch of guys I work with." Scotty barked laughter too much like Reggie's. "Used to work with. Doing odd jobs no one else wants, cleaning up messes not near as bad as the one I'm in. They all stayed in a duplex on the edge of town, run down dump of a place. Anyway, had trouble with all of them at one time or another. You know how it is."

Reggie did know. Scotty had had *trouble* with almost everyone in his life from the time he was in grade school. His bedroom walls weren't the only thing he'd tried to beat to death.

"So I heard from our boss, the one we did the odd jobs for. Said these guys told him I was stealing from him. Taking money off the top of what I collected, keeping things I'd picked up for myself. Whatever else I am, I ain't a damn thief. I asked a couple of them and of course they denied it. But they never did have a good word to say about me."

Scotty paused, then blew out his breath loud enough to make the phone rumble. Reggie saw his son in his mind then, just as he'd been when he left but bigger. More filled out. Sitting back in his chair, legs crossed with his ankle on his knee. Brown hair spiked up, half-smoked cigarette in one hand no matter how much his parents begged and threatened. Reggie smelled the menthol and tobacco smoke so strongly he fought back a cough.

"They were all supposed to be on a job out of town," Scotty said. "Boss told me that's why he had me doing grunt work that day, because they were all gone. Well, like an idiot I believed him. I drove over there that night, splashed gas on the siding and dead bushes, and lit the place up. I was too angry to think straight, I guess. Didn't check to see if they were actually home."

"But they were."

"Sound asleep. No smoke detectors in the place, or maybe they were too drunk to hear them. I didn't even know until the next day. That's when I panicked and called you. Arson in Texas is bad enough. Once you throw murder on top of it, you're talking a first degree felony. That's the rest of my life in prison, but they might love the death penalty down here enough to try that, see if it sticks. Got to head south and stay there."

"The gas in the car," Reggie said, his voice weak.

"What?"

"That's why I smelled gas. I thought it was a fuel leak. In the car."

"I didn't even notice that. Taking the heap up to Ohio might really help me out, then. You should take it on to a junkyard where it belongs. Or push it into the river."

Reggie nodded, aware Scotty couldn't see him, but with no idea what he was agreeing with. His heart pounded in his ears, his body ran hot and cold. His brain so sluggish he might as well be drugged.

His son. This was his son.

No matter how things had turned out, this was the laughing little baby who'd held on to his pinkie finger so tight it hurt. The smiling toddler who giggled madly as he ran off every chance he got. The little boy who loved nothing more than cuddling up between his parents when they were watching TV.

That boy had grown into a man, and that man was a murderer. The only thing Scotty seemed to feel bad about was that he might get caught if he didn't run far enough.

"Yeah, probably should junk it," Reggie said. "Not much else to do. Junk it and everything else."

He squeezed his temples with his fingers and thumb, trying to make sense of anything inside his skull.

Could he walk away and pretend this never happened? Force himself to forget what he knew, never tell another person as long as he lived? Let Scotty run off to Mexico and hope to never hear from him again? Hope that was far enough that he never heard of anything else Scotty did, no matter how bad?

The hell was Reggie didn't know if that would be easier to live with than turning Scotty in. Sending his only child to prison.

"That sure would help me out," Scotty said. "Biggest mess I've got myself into since the old woman's statues or dolls or whatever she called them."

Reggie's heart stopped, then lurched painfully in his chest.

"The old woman? You mean your grandmother?"

"Yeah, don't you remember that? Thought Mom was going to hold me down so Grandma could kill me." He cackled again. "Death by old lady."

Reggie remembered. More than he could stand to deal with while Scotty was on the phone. He held his breath for a few seconds, then forced himself to start talking.

"You need money, son? I can get my hands on a little bit. A few thousand."

"Course I need money. I didn't exactly have time to plan ahead for this great escape."

"Listen, I know you don't have a lot of time. Are you close enough to get here tonight? I can leave it in the glove box. I'd rather see you, maybe take you out for a decent meal, but in case you can't stop."

"I...yeah. I can get there. By sunrise for sure. I'd hate to wake you up, long drive tomorrow and all."

Reggie swallowed hard, checking himself over inside and out. Trying to decide if he could go through with this.

"I understand, son. I have to run out and find an ATM, but that shouldn't even take an hour. I'll get out as much as I can. Remember the name of the place?"

"Well great! Yeah, I remember. You really came through for me, Dad. I'll try to make it in time to say goodbye."

This time, Reggie ended the call himself. The hard calm surging through his mind and body scared him, but he knew he'd use it as long as it lasted.

He gathered up all his things, then drove the heap about five minutes to a bank he'd spotted on the way in. He drew out a few hundred dollars in twenties, enough to look good in a bundle. And enough to bribe the motel clerk to check him out early, call a taxi to the airport, and keep his mouth shut.

Reggie left the money and the pager in the glove box and dropped the key in a drain grate on the other side of the parking lot.

He waited out the drive to the airport, the same one he'd flown into. Ten minutes with no traffic.

Out on the curb, he used the cheap phone to call the police. Anonymous tip, easiest thing in the world.

Yes, he thought the arson suspect would be at the hotel sometime in the next few hours.

No, he didn't have anything else to say.

The phone's battery went into a garbage can. The phone went into the bottom of his suitcase, soon to end its days at the bottom of a river in Ohio.

The last flight out was in a couple of hours, but Reggie thought that would work out just fine. He didn't know if anything else ever would.

All he knew was he was thankful all the damn voices in his head kept their opinions to themselves for a change.

First thing when he got home, he'd go visit his mother-in-law. Former, technically, but Reggie never felt like he divorced her. He never wanted to. She'd been a thousand times the mother to him than his own managed, even when her memory started to go.

Her most prized possession in all her homes and in her room at the assisted living was her collection of figurines. Silly little things. Pastel painted girls and boys, cats and dogs. A couple dozen or so, carefully collected throughout her life. She always wanted them lined up where she could see them first thing when she woke up.

A few years ago, those figurines had turned up broken when she was out at a doctor's appointment. Not only knocked off, but smashed. Ground into the rug with someone's heel from the looks of it.

Reggie's wife had insisted she'd handle it with the staff herself.

Reggie had insisted on sitting with his mother-in-law that night and again the next day. Her soft, childlike crying wrecked him, breaking his heart more than the day his own mother died. He held her hands as she whispered *why* over and over again.

Scotty ran off less than a week later.

Reggie paced around his nearly empty departure gate, orbiting his suitcase.

The kid had a decent chance still. If he got there sooner than the cops, he might get away.

Get away with it.

Again.

Or he might not.

That was up to him and up to fate.

Reggie vowed to do everything in his power to never find out.

GRIEF SPAM

KRISTINE KATHRYN RUSCH

I've edited numerous mystery anthologies, including The Best Mystery and Crime Stories. *I am the former editor of* The Magazine of Fantasy & Science Fiction *as well as many other projects. As a mystery writer, I've been nominated for the Edgar and Shamus awards. I've won the Ellery Queen Reader's Choice Award, and been nominated for several other awards. My Smokey Dalton series, written under the name Kris Nelscott, is an international bestselling series.*

"Grief Spam" came from an article I read about those horrible people who actually prey on grieving people. Apparently, computer programs comb the death notices and send spam to families in mourning. I was going to write an angry revealing story about spam. Instead, this emerged. I hope you enjoy it.

Day sixteen since Rob's death, not that Lucca was counting—oh, hell, of course she was counting. The days, the hours, the minutes. She was counting everything because that was the only way to keep her brain focused.

But not focused well enough apparently, because she woke up that morning, like she had for the past fifteen mornings, reaching for Rob on his side of the bed, wondering why he had gotten up so early, wondering what day it was, wondering if she had forgotten to drive him to work, wondering—

And then she remembered. Sledgehammer, nightmare, emotionally devastating.

Those words didn't even describe it.

More like existing between being and nothingness. She rested on the soft king bed, pillow scrunched beneath her head, covers wrapped around her like a hug, the cats pressed against her as if they were afraid she would leave too, and let the reality sink in.

She used a trick, one she had developed ten days ago. She reviewed everything in her head.

She started with the obit, because she had had to write it, and she had the damn thing memorized:

Robert Zedder, 48, loving father and husband, died in a single car collision on Route 73, just outside Watersville. Beloved assistant principal of Anderson High School, Zedder had worked for the Watersville School District for twenty-five years. Recipient of Teacher of the Year for five years running, Zedder maintained his teaching career while working in the high school administration.

He leaves behind his wife, Lucca Kwindale, his daughters Annette, Sybil Washington, and Marla Zedder-James, and three granddaughters...

At which point, Lucca's throat ached—every single time. He would never see Annette graduate from college, never see the grandbabies grow, never see their babies, never see—

Lucca made herself sit up. The cats lifted their heads, startled, bits of their fur floating in the semi-light of the early morning filtering in the bedroom window. A bedroom on the east side of the house had been Rob's idea, since he had to get up early for school. Too early, she had always complained, and he would laugh.

Self-employed people don't understand schedules, he would say, and by that he would mean *she* didn't understand schedules, never realizing that self-employed people had to schedule better than anybody else, or no one would think they were working.

Old arguments, now irrelevant. Lucca ran a hand over her face. Day sixteen. He had died on a Tuesday (a Tuesday in April, four days before taxes were due, at four in the goddamn morning—what had he been doing driving at four in the goddamn morning?), which meant that this was Thursday, some mucky-muck day at the end of April, nearly May, which he used to say was his favorite month.

Mucky-muck day. She'd learned that phrase from him too. She had lived half her life with him—married at twenty-four—and she was having trouble separating herself from that. Having trouble figuring out how to move forward, how to think, even. Strangely, it had been easier in the first few days after his death because there had been—ironically enough—a schedule.

So, last night, she realized she needed a new schedule. The nonexistent schedule, she would have said to him, had he still been alive, and she would have said it with a smile, and just enough sarcasm and bite to let him know she kinda resented the way he had minimized her work each and every day.

He would have heard the bite, and it would have made him defensive.

He was helping people, he would have said, teaching kids how to be good citizens, making sure the school ran well, working toward the future.

He hated her work. She didn't hate his, but she thought it was dreary.

She didn't see her work as noble—only private detectives in novels were noble—but she saw it as useful and interesting, and a whole hell of a lot less dangerous now that she did 90% of it online.

She and her crew. Her crew, who were taking point at the moment. Her crew, who probably needed some kind of pep-talk acknowledgment from her.

Later today, she would head to the office where the crew worked. She would give them an hour. She figured she could handle an hour without tears. Maybe an hour would give her enough focus to put her pesky emotions in their place.

She'd read about grief. Hell, she'd combed the web to find out everything she could about grief.

It's a process, the websites told her.

It's harder when things are left unsaid, the websites warned.

Be aware, they counseled. *The emotions come in waves.*

Emotion*s*, not emotion. Not sadness, not mind-numbing despair. But sadness *and* mind-numbing despair. Anger *and* denial. Shock *and* acceptance. Depression *and* bargaining—wait. Bargaining with whom? With the idiot who was out driving at four in the morning on a school night? Who probably fell asleep behind the goddamn wheel, missed a turn, and slammed into a concrete abutment that was slated to be repaired by the Department of Transportation next summer, because the damn abutment was an accident magnet?

Whew. She let out a small breath. Anger. It billowed when she least expected it. She didn't think of herself as an angry person, but she certainly wasn't a calm one either.

Never had been, never would be.

She had made a list the night before, so she wouldn't have to think about her day. Thinking about the day, she believed, was what had paralyzed her this past week. Now that the funeral was over. Now that the girls had gone home to their separate cities, their separate lives, and their separate grief. Now that the planning was done.

Yeah, right. The lack of schedule had paralyzed her. Not the loss of Rob. Not that at all.

Lucca grabbed her robe from the chair beside the bed, slipped her feet into the worn slippers she'd meant to replace at Christmas, made a brief stop in the bathroom, avoided the kitchen where the cats were already gathering for their breakfast treats, and proceeded down the side hall to her home office.

A second master the builders had called it when they slapped this place together from custom pieces. She didn't care about what they called this part of the house. When she and Rob had looked for the perfect home to raise their family in, she had insisted on the home office, as far from the main living quarters as possible.

She just wanted—and got— two rooms and a bathroom to herself so she could have an outer office and an inner sanctuary. She even had her own entrance—very important in the early days, when (stupidly) she let the clients come here.

She had never told Rob about the guy who had threatened her at knife point, or the cheating wife who had shown up with a shaking gun in her right hand. Rob couldn't have done anything about it except worry. In his later years, he had put on weight around the middle, always intending to exercise, and never exercising at all.

If he had been alone with someone who had become violent

because of her work, he wouldn't have been able to defend himself. He would have died, because of her. (Of course, this year, he had died because of him. Or the damn abutment. Or the stupid car.)

It had taken a knife and a gun, and a couple of threats left on her voice mail to wake her up. Fortunately, before anything had happened.

Before someone had gone after her family with evil intent.

That year—ten years ago now—Lucca had decided on an outside office, the farther away the better. Rob had complained bitterly, about the distance, the expense, the location—everything. Initially she thought he was being controlling—he didn't want her away from the house. Later, she thought maybe the outside office made her work even more embarrassing to him.

He thought of private detectives as blue collar. He'd once said, *What a waste of an education, Lucca. You were Phi Beta Kappa, second in a class of five hundred at one of the most prestigious universities in the nation. I tell my kids they want to achieve all those goals so they'll get the best jobs ever, not dig through someone else's underwear to see if it has holes.*

She'd walked away from him that day. Hadn't even fought back. They'd said a lot of ugly things to each other in their fights, but neither of them had ever walked away before.

And he knew—because he wasn't dumb (wasn't Phi Beta Kappa either, but wasn't dumb)—that if he kept pushing her like that, she would walk away for good.

So she'd got her outside office. Smartest decision she'd ever made, besides going back to school to learn the ins and outs of computer research. As the business grew, the offices grew, the staff grew, and she out-earned Rob by more than double.

Although, since she handled the family finances, he never knew that. He hadn't known a lot of things, because she'd stopped telling him.

There had been no point.

And now, he would never know. Her legs buckled at the thought. She put a hand on the wall, wondered if, now that he was dead, he actually did know. Maybe he knew everything now. Some cultures believed that consciousness spread all over time, learning life's lessons.

She made herself stand up, let go of the wall, keep moving. She wasn't a weak person, no matter how she felt. She wasn't superhero strong, either, but she could move forward in the face of all difficulties.

Rob'd said once, after Annette was born, that he thought Lucca could give birth, then take a five-mile hike, and cook a six-course meal, all in the same day.

She didn't have that kind of stamina now—in fact, she couldn't remember the last time he had said something like that—but she was usually stronger than she had been these past sixteen days. Not the kind of woman who sobbed alone in her bedroom, with only her cats for company.

Lucca opened the hallway door into her office. The door led into the outer sanctum, once the reception, now a dump spot for old paper files, boxes, and photographs that should probably never see the light of day.

The inner office remained her home office, six different kinds of computers and two laptops, three routers, all hard-wired in, plus two different internet hot spots through two different companies. She did searches here that she didn't want on her office network, and she routinely cleaned off and dumped computers when she had stumbled on some truly perverted stuff in the course of an investigation.

Usually she used the client's computer for that, going through whatever they let her investigate, sometimes in her office, sometimes in their home. But she'd been doing this long enough that she got a sense of people, and she could tell if they were the kind who might make her life a living hell.

In the middle of the computer jungle was her personal laptop, the one she used for family emails and her private social media accounts—the ones only shared with her daughters, her extended family, and a handful of close friends. She made sure she bought a new laptop every year, something cheap and not very sophisticated, and carried it with her on vacations and in the car.

She liked to think of that computer as an extension of the woman who lived in this house, the woman who had married Rob, bore three children, and raised them in as old-fashioned a way possible. Sometimes she thought of that woman as the fictional version of herself, the one she presented to the family and to the neighborhood, not the hard-assed broad who knew when a client was lying to her, or who had talked down that guy with a knife.

She grabbed the computer out of her old leather recliner, the one piece of furniture in the entire house that predated everything, from her relationship with Rob to the move to this city. An old boyfriend had bought the chair for her, the only piece of furniture in her entire one-bedroom apartment. She'd slept in the damn chair for nearly three months, long after he had broken up with her.

Rob hadn't known where the chair came from, only that she wouldn't part with it because it had been in her first apartment. He hadn't asked more.

She sank into it, robe parting along her knees. She cradled the laptop to her chest, thinking about her future while all wrapped up in her past.

Well-made furniture often outlived the people who first owned it. Well-built houses did too. Stuff lived longer than people, than husbands, than true love.

Sometimes stuff held its secrets—like this chair—secrets that would die with her. And sometimes stuff broadcast the secrets far and wide, once the stuff had been found in a hidden compartment or in the back of a closet or tucked (forgotten) in the pocket of an old coat.

She used to love ironies like that.

She used to love a lot of things.

She shook off the thought, opened her laptop, and typed in her password. The screen bounced into life, informing her that she hadn't opened the laptop in seventeen days—a notification she set up for herself so that she would know when she'd neglected her personal life for much too long.

Seventeen days.

He'd been dead for sixteen.

She couldn't remember why she had been on the computer the day before his death. Probably checking Facebook, seeing what the girls were doing, looking at the pictures of her grandbabies, or maybe even downloading music for her marathon exercise sessions.

It all blurred.

She took a deep breath before opening her email program. She knew what she would find. Dozens (maybe hundreds) of condolences. Lots of offers of help—whatever that meant. Grief spam (a widowed friend had warned her about that). And way back, normal emails, the kind that had been sent Before, the kind that had assumed normal would continue, not just for hours, but for days, months, and years.

She clicked on the computer's built-in timer, set it for an hour, then opened the email program. One hour. If she didn't want to read the condolence letters she didn't have to. She could just spend that hour deleting the grief spam.

The email downloaded faster than she expected. Three hundred emails, according to the little bar, most of them from familiar names. She watched the subject lines change from mundane things to topics like *Thinking of You* and *Call Us If You Need Anything*.

And then, in the middle of it, emails from people she didn't recognize, with the subject lines in all caps.

THE TRUTH ABOUT ROBERT ZEDDER; SEE WHAT ROBERT ZEDDER HAD DONE IN THE DAYS LEADING UP TO HIS DEATH; DISCOVER WHO ROBERT ZEDDER REALLY WAS.

On and on and on. That wasn't the grief spam she had been expecting. She had expected (and gotten) *Meditation for Widows* (Jesus, she was a widow now), *Join Our Grief Community*, and *Avoid Scams Targeted at the Grieving* (she thought that particularly pernicious).

But the ones with Robert's name, those disturbed her.

She looked at the dates of the emails, saw they had come to her after the obituary was published (every-damn-where), and slammed the laptop closed.

GRIEF SPAM

Fucking predators. That was a particular kind of nasty that she would delete when she was calm enough. When she wasn't feeling like isolating and opening each email before sending malware directly to the sender. When she wasn't feeling like tracking down the IP and finding the person's exact address, and going there and—

She made herself breathe, again.

She set the laptop aside and stood. The timer would go off, but it wouldn't repeat, so she could just leave it.

She needed breakfast anyway.

After that, the kitchen felt like a haven, rather than a reminder of Rob's absence. Even though his favorite shoes sat haphazardly under the table in the breakfast nook, where he had taken them off the night before. Even though his nasty protein powders still cluttered up her granite countertop. Even though the mail was piled a bit too high on the island.

Light poured into the windows that surrounded the nook, and outside, leaves had sprouted on the trees that gave this part of the lawn so much privacy.

The three cats twirled and meowed on the tile floor, waiting for her to take care of them, which she did—the standard morning routine, the same as it had been a month ago—filling bowls, filling water, giving them a bit of soft food.

She followed the routine, because she had promised herself routine, poured some shredded wheat, dressed it up with fresh strawberries someone had left, added a side of peanut butter toast for protein, took her damn vitamins, and made coffee.

Routine.

Except she couldn't turn on the TV under the counter, couldn't open her tablet to see the news of the day, couldn't bear to do more than stare and eat. Finally, she picked up her phone, tapped it open —and found nearly a dozen texts and messages from her daughters.

The most recent came from Antoinette.

Mom! Where Are You?

Followed by one from Marla.

Mom, we're getting concerned.

And from Sybil.
Mother, you need to pick up the phone.

Lucca scrolled through before she did, not willing to be blindsided by anything, but afraid she might be.

Her phone vibrated in her hand. She had shut off the ringer days ago. The screen lit up: the call was from Antoinette.

Lucca leaned against the kitchen island, bracing herself, gaze on the empty cat dishes still littering the floor, and answered the phone.

"Hey, baby girl," she said, as she always did when greeting her youngest.

"Mom. Where *were* you?" Antoinette's voice hadn't shaken like that since she was six, and broke her leg after falling out of a tree.

"I—um—." Lucca glanced at the clock on the microwave. It was eleven-thirty, much later than she usually got up. "I have been keeping the phone in the kitchen."

She had expected Antoinette to say something about that, but she didn't. Instead, Antoinette took an audibly shaky breath, and said,

"They're not true, are they? Those screen shots? They're made up, right?"

Screen shots? Lucca felt dizzy. Outside of the house, Rob was alive, handling the kids at school with his usual mixture of aplomb, severity, and humor, taking the small emergencies. He would have handled this, this call, the girls upset. He would have dealt with it, because he handled kids. All the kids.

"What screen shots?" Lucca asked, wishing she didn't have to.

"You haven't *seen* them? Mom, aren't you getting your email?"

Lucca's breakfast rolled in her stomach. Those emails—they had gone to her daughters.

"I downloaded it," Lucca said, "but didn't look at it."

Not really. Just enough to see those subject lines—*The Truth About Robert Zedder.*

The truth.

"You have to look, Mom." Antoinette's voice wobbled. "You have to do *something*. It can't be about Dad. It can't."

"It probably isn't," Lucca said as calmly as she could manage—more calmly than she expected, in fact. She was talking to her daughter now as if Antoinette were an unruly client. "A widowed friend of mine warned me about the email. She called it grief spam."

"And you didn't warn us?" Antoinette asked. "You should have warned us."

"I didn't think you'd get any," Lucca said. *I didn't think it would be personal, either,* she wanted to add. *With Rob's name and everything.* "I'll text your sisters and then take a look."

"It's awful, Mom," Antoinette said.

"I'll keep that in mind," Lucca said, and hung up.

She texted her other two daughters and told them to hold tight; she was investigating. They knew that investigating was one of Lucca's most serious words.

Then she headed back down the hall, clutching the phone, and bracing herself. Antoinette said the spam was awful, but it couldn't be worse than identifying Rob's body through that stupid camera at the morgue, or looking at his embalmed but broken face, and calmly agreeing with the mortician that the casket should remain closed.

Lucca was braced—and weirdly, a little relieved. Something to do. Not make-work. Not work for the sake of work.

Something that mattered. For her girls.

Lucca set the phone on the side of her big desk, then grabbed the laptop off her leather chair. She pulled back her desk chair, and sat down, placing the laptop in the center of all the equipment.

She'd done this kind of work a million times before. She knew how to look at sensitive information on someone's personal laptop. She was just going to pretend this laptop wasn't hers.

Lucca isolated the laptop. For the moment, it didn't have to be attached to any internet connection; she had already downloaded the email.

Then she tugged her robe tightly closed, leaned forward, and opened her email program.

There were more of those grief spam emails than she had thought. Before she even opened them, she glanced at who had sent them. She didn't recognize the name on the account, but the actual address used to send the email had a dodgy URL. She didn't go there. She had another system she would use for that, or maybe, if things weren't as bad as she feared, she would report the URL to the office, and let her staff work on this.

She paused over the Rob-specific emails. There were at least a dozen of them, maybe more if she checked her spam filter, which she wasn't ready to do yet. Whoever had set up the subject line had done so with care, so that the emails *wouldn't* get caught in the spam filter.

Her hesitation was not unusual. She needed to figure out how best to deal with these emails.

But if she had been opening the emails in real time, rather than ignoring her personal laptop altogether, she would have opened a few one day, and more the next.

So the best thing she could do was open these emails in chronological order.

She let out a small breath. Whoever had sent these emails had waited more than a week for her to open them, and then, when she hadn't, had sent email to her daughters.

Had she not been an investigator, she would have immediately thought that all of this was personal. But her daughters were listed in the obituary, and anyone with a computer and the sense of a half-wit could find them.

Lucca's mouth was dry, and she wished she had grabbed her coffee. But she hadn't. Then she clicked on the first email—received a day or so (maybe hours) after the obituary was published.

The Truth About Robert Zedder! The interior screamed, just like a headline.

Then it quoted the obituary—loving father and husband— with several attached pictures underneath the words.

The pictures were what she expected. Blurry images of a man who might or might not be Rob, kissing a woman who was definitely not Lucca.

Lucca could fake up this sort of thing in less than fifteen minutes.

She could search for the images on the internet and see where they were pulled from, and maybe even identify the couple.

But she didn't.

Instead, she opened the next email.

It had a subject line similar to the one she had just looked at, and the format was the same. Only this one was focused on "loving father." Again, blurry photos, clearly obscene and awful, with a man and a girl who couldn't have been more than eight.

The man might've been Rob. But he might've been any other dark-haired middle-aged tubby white guy.

This stuff was generic, disgusting and hideous, designed to upset the recipient. But Lucca had seen worse, much worse, from people she had thought she had known. Those upset her.

This was a poor attempt at—what, exactly?

She couldn't find anything that stated a purpose in the email. Not a link, not a request for money, not a claim of blackmail, nothing.

It looked like someone was trying to destroy Rob's reputation, but surely, anyone who would want to do that would know that Rob's wife was a private investigator and would be able to figure out who had sent the emails.

Or maybe it was some kid at the high school who had hated Rob, and decided to get revenge on his family.

Lucca let out a small breath. That thought made her feel a little unclean. It would take a special kind of budding young sociopath to come up with something like this.

But this could be an entire blackmail campaign, with the ask at the end. The fact that there were a dozen or more of these things led her to believe that inside these emails would be some kind of escalation—she just wasn't sure what it would be.

She backed up her email program and all of the emails on two different thumb drives, just in case opening one of the other emails would destroy her entire computer. Such things happened a lot to her clients, and her team was usually called in too late to deal with the mess.

While the program was copying onto the thumb drives, Lucca

used time to take a quick shower (first time in two days!), put on the jeans and denim shirt she had laid out the night before, heat up some coffee, and grab one of the chocolate banana muffins someone had given her.

The orgy of food had been amazing right after Rob's death, and Lucca had expected it to slow down, but since she wasn't communicating (much) with her friends, they had taken to leaving food baskets on her doorstep.

People were worried about her, and she found that both touching and irritating and, at the moment, highly convenient.

She walked back into the inner sanctum just as the laptop bonged its little *I'm done!* sound. She pulled the thumb drives and labeled them, setting them near her phone as something to deal with later.

Her phone's screen flared on, showing four more texts from her daughters, getting more and more insistent.

Lucca couldn't ignore them, not with the girls so very upset. So, she sent a group text to all three of them, telling them to calm down —she had this—and then went back to work.

The next two emails were just as generic as the first two. Then the tone of the emails changed.

See What Rob Zedder Did In The Days Before His Death! emails actually had photographs of Rob, taken primarily off security cameras from convenience stores, traffic cameras, and bank systems.

She felt a flash of irritated responsibility—she was going to have to let all of those organizations know they had been compromised.

Then she sipped her coffee, which was already tepid, crammed part of the banana muffin into her mouth (more chocolate than banana, and good), and looked at the first *What Rob Did* email more closely, to see why the anonymous emailer thought these would be upsetting.

She couldn't see anything upsetting, even when she made the emails larger. She didn't click on the photographs, though. She would click links and photographs after she had finished the initial glance at the emails.

She was about to give up on that particular series of emails when she figured out what was wrong: the time stamps on each photo—and they all had time stamps, because they were from security cameras—were in the middle of the day, when Rob was supposed to be at the high school.

Her first inclination—her investigator's inclination—was to call the school to see if Rob had actually been at work at those times on those days. But that could wait. Because she still didn't know the purpose of these emails, and she didn't want to be manipulated into any kind of unusual behavior.

The next three emails were simple threats with varying degrees of menace. The upshot of each? *We have more information on Robert Zedder* and the implication was that they would release that information, ruin Rob's reputation, and destroy everyone's belief in him.

But for what gain? She couldn't find that, not yet.

That was beginning to bother her.

Finally, she got to the last three emails. They all had the subject header *Discover Who Robert Zedder Really Was*, but the headline in each email was different.

The first said, *You Think You Knew Robert Zedder. You Were Wrong.*

Buried into the body of the email were more pictures. Only these were screen shots. The first series appeared to be screen shots from SnapChat on someone's phone. The snippet of conversation, from almost a month ago, would have been disappeared by now—stuff remained on Snapchat for only twenty-four hours or so—but someone had thought to preserve it.

And augment it.

One of the handles—midfindotdlegercom—had a computer-drawn fake-handwritten scrawl next to it, identifying it as Rob's. The posts were nasty, vicious, hate-filled, calling out someone for being transgender. Lucca wouldn't have believed it was Rob at all, except that she recognized the handle.

Rob loved using parts of words in a patterned repeat. He had taught her that trick back in the days when passwords didn't need numbers and punctuation. This particular handle came from the words *Middle Finger Dot Com*. (*Mid-Fin-Dot-Dle-Ger-Com*).

Her phone vibrated across the desk. She glanced at the laptop's clock, realized she'd been working for nearly two hours. That call had to be from one of her daughters.

Lucca picked up the phone, glanced at the screen, but didn't answer. The caller had been Marla this time.

I'm still working on it, Lucca texted all three of them. She didn't tell them she had only just gotten to the screenshots.

Given Antoinette's text earlier that morning, the three girls suspected these messages were from Rob as well. He had probably taught them the same trick that he had taught Lucca.

She made herself focus, rather than think about how her daughters were feeling. Right now, they were just clients, and she was going to treat them that way.

Treating them that way enabled her to keep her distance from this, so that she didn't think about her husband, Rob. Instead, she was focusing on some guy named Rob, who might or might not have been a pig on Snapchat.

Although the screenshots weren't just from Snapchat, but from other apps that provided "privacy," deleting messages some time after they were posted. There were even a few screenshots from Facebook's Messenger app, the special feature that also made messages disappear.

And none of the posts were nice. All of them were nasty, trollish, horrid pieces—taking apart gays, African-Americans, and women. Vicious, hideous stuff, the kind of things that Rob The Saintly would have told her that he didn't want "his kids" saying in school.

With some trepidation, Lucca opened the last email.

She had expected some kind of ask or a request to go to a website or a demand for money so none of this would go out.

And there was none.

Just two sentences:

Aren't you happy to be rid of that asshole now? You really should thank me.

And then, nothing.

Nothing at all.

GRIEF SPAM

She had to stand up after reading those two lines. She grabbed the last part of the muffin, ate it without really thinking about it, and chased it with the remains of the coffee.

Then she went into the kitchen to get more.

She was fully aware that she was dealing with her sudden stress by shoving it down with food. Which was better than what she had been doing all week, which had been avoiding food, except when her body reminded her.

She grabbed another chocolate-banana muffin, poured more coffee, thought for a brief minute about actually putting something healthy in her body, and then decided against it.

She was working. It shouldn't matter that she was working on something about Rob. She needed to act as if she hadn't met him at all.

Although, if she hadn't met him, she would think he had written all of that crap in the screenshots. She might even consider that he had done the stuff in the blurry photos.

She shuddered. If she had spent years sharing her bed—her life— with a creature like the one in "loving father" then she should be indicted herself.

She didn't even remember sitting down in her leather chair. One moment she was in the kitchen, the next she was checking her spam filter. There had to be an ask, somewhere. Or a demand. Something to make this effort worthwhile to the sender.

She didn't find it in the spam filter or in the junk folder. She checked through the email again to see if she had missed something.

She hadn't.

Could it be that the person who had sent these emails hadn't wanted a response from her? Had they sent emails to her daughters because the barrage that came to Lucca was done? Were they trying to convince the family that Rob wasn't the person they had thought he was?

Lucca stood, remembering Antoinette's voice, shaking like it had when she was six. Seeing the texts from all three of her daughters: *Mom, those screenshots aren't real. Are they?*

Already the doubt. Already the worry.

Some poison had wormed its way into Lucca's family—and she wasn't sure how to get it out.

First things, first, though. She had to find out what her daughters had received. She texted them, telling them to forward the emails to her personal laptop account rather than any business account, like she would have if they were clients.

She figured the laptop account was already compromised—hell the laptop itself might've been compromised—so she was just trying to contain the problem into one space.

Besides, she was trying to act like a client would. If someone was monitoring the online communications—as Rob's wife, not as Lucca Kwindale, private investigator—they would expect the daughters to forward their emails. A healthy family would work together, and Lucca's family had been healthy.

Hadn't it?

She rubbed a hand over her face. It would be so easy to blame the grief or the exhaustion on her emotional roller coaster, but that wasn't entirely why she was having doubts.

There had always been parts of Rob she hadn't understood, and as he had gotten older, parts she hadn't liked. They were a true mismatch, the kind that happened when people got married too young.

She hadn't left because of the girls, although she had been toying with it now that Antoinette was nearly out of college. The household hadn't had to remain stable, she had been thinking, and she had seen no reason to live in the big house with a man she wasn't really sure she would have talked to if they had met now.

Lucca gathered the crumbs of the second muffin, not remembering consuming all of it. She dribbled them into her mouth like a teenager.

She had been dealing with those thoughts—the thoughts of divorce, of leaving—ever since Rob had died. She hadn't told anyone about that, not because she felt guilty, but because she didn't.

Maybe that was why the doubts had come so fast. She hadn't liked him, not the man he had become.

But it was a stretch to think he had skipped out of work and even more of a stretch to think he had written all of those nasty things on all of those social media sites.

She wiped off her fingers, sipped even more coffee, and went back to work. She had a moment of trepidation as she attached the laptop to her dedicated internet line. She half expected the laptop to freeze up, or ransom ware to appear, but nothing like that happened.

She downloaded the email, then immediately went offline. She would do the other work—going to the websites and links—later, depending on what she found.

She isolated her daughters' emails by daughter, wondering if they got different emails. Lucca started with Marla's because she was the eldest. She was also the most visible of the children, and ostensibly, the one with the most money. If Lucca were doing this horrid thing, she would have gone to the wife first, and then getting no response, to the eldest child, and worked her way down.

But if Lucca had been doing this horrid thing, she would have asked for money to keep the damn information off the streets, rather than sending that pointed final email.

The emails weren't quite the same. First, Marla hadn't received all twelve. She had only received seven—although Lucca would ask her to double-check her spam filters.

The first three were exactly the same, including the hideous "loving father" email. There was only one in the middle, with photos showing Rob coming out of a hotel, photos taken by the security camera of a bank. Lucca had received those photos as well.

The last three were different, though. They were screenshots, yes, but they were from private chat boards. The handle was the same as on the ones she received— midfindotdlegercom—and Rob's name had been "written" in the same red lettering as on her screenshots.

But these were worse than Lucca's. Not in political content, but in personal content. They would dig directly into Marla's self-esteem.

I got "blessed" with three daughters, one of the posts read, *and all of them take after my wife, who is no prize, let me tell you. I was happy to have married the oldest daughter off, because she made bitchiness her life's work. Couldn't wait for her to move out.*

And another:

Don't get your girlfriend pregnant, no matter what you do. If I'd used a condom, I wouldn't have been "blessed" with the Bitch Queen of the Universe as a daughter.

Lucca took her hands off the keyboard. She stepped away from the laptop, because if she didn't, she would put her fist through the screen.

Those posts were Rob's. She knew it as clearly as if she had heard him say those things.

One of his favorite sayings was "Bitch Queen of the Universe," only he'd used it to describe a woman he worked with, as well as the Watersville's mayor. Lucca had never heard him use it to describe his daughters, though. Although he hadn't really liked Marla.

He'd said that to Lucca many times over the years, always in a perplexed way. *Isn't a father supposed to fall in love with his child?* he'd ask.

The question was plaintive in the beginning, then biting later. He'd actually talked about getting a DNA test when Marla was thirteen and difficult. The subtext was—always had been with her—that she was Lucca's fault.

Lucca, for not being on the pill. Lucca, for refusing to terminate the pregnancy. Lucca, for trapping him into marriage—even though he had been the one to ask her. She had told him, more than once, that she was perfectly willing to raise the baby alone.

And that was the thing that bothered her the most. Only two people knew that Lucca had been pregnant when she got married.

GRIEF SPAM

They hadn't lived near family at the time, so they had "eloped," going to Vegas for a quickie wedding.

She had been four months pregnant, but not showing from the angles of the photographs they had taken. That had been July. Marla had been born in December. And with her birth announcement, they had included the announcement of their marriage, changing the date so that it seemed like they had gotten married in March instead.

Her parents had been wounded that Lucca hadn't had a traditional wedding, but they had known that their middle child had never been a traditional person. His parents were crushed, and that was when the blaming had started.

If only I had worn a condom, he would say until finally Lucca had shushed him.

You keep saying that and when the baby gets older, she'll have a complex, Lucca said.

She had been a young twenty-four when she married him, still naïve enough to believe that two parents were better than one, idealistic enough to think that love (even pallid love, like theirs) would survive anything, hopeful enough to believe that a second child would make things better, and tired enough to figure out that a third child wouldn't make that much difference—especially when she, like her oldest sister, hadn't been planned.

Lucca glanced at her phone. No texts now, except one from her office.

Call when you're feeling up to it, her office manager wrote.

Lucca certainly wasn't feeling up to it at the moment. If she talked to anyone, she'd bite their head off.

She sat back down.

Time to find out if her other daughters had gotten similar emails.

Time to find out exactly what the hell was going on here.

Both Sybil and Antoinette had received seven emails, and four of them were exactly the same as the ones Marla and Lucca had received. But the last three were different in each case, personal, and nasty.

And clearly written by Rob.

The things he had written about Sybil and the fact that she had embraced the traditional values of her husband were breathtakingly vicious. Compound that with the slurs Rob wrote about Sybil's conversion to Catholicism, and the devastation was complete.

Lucca's heart ached for her daughter, who didn't deserve any of that, no matter how holier-than-thou she had gotten when Rob confronted her years ago.

He hadn't liked any religion, not deep down.

Maybe Lucca should have had that religious funeral after all, not as a sop to Sybil, but as a fuck-you to Rob.

If only Lucca could do it all over again.

She hesitated before opening Antoinette's emails. Sybil and Marla were women full-grown, and they had their own families who loved them, and could help them through this.

But Antoinette had just broken up with her girlfriend, and had had to move out just the week before Rob died. Antoinette had been fragile then, losing a love she had thought would be permanent.

Lucca couldn't quite imagine how her daughter felt now.

Particularly since half the stuff Rob had said about her had been ugly too. The homophobic slurs that Lucca had received in her three emails appeared in Antoinette's emails, and they seemed worse, because they were actually combined with some kind of weird empathy.

I got a butch daughter, one of the comments read. *She's perfect except for her predilections. I'd thought she was the daughter of my dreams until I realized she had this flaw. I know without asking that the bitch-wife won't tolerate any kind of conversion therapy, so we gotta live with a near-perfect child who is going to destroy her entire future by either being too butch to ever get a high-end job or being too focused on politics to do good work at whatever job she does get.*

Lucca's lower lip trembled. A tear ran down her cheek, but she

GRIEF SPAM

wasn't mourning anymore. She wasn't grief-angry anymore either. She was sad for her daughters.

Who would do this to them? They didn't need to know how their father had actually felt.

Lucca had known about some of his feelings, but not all of them. And she had never put them together into such a vile package.

She had no idea what she would say to her girls.

Aren't you happy to be rid of that asshole now? the emails asked.

If it had just been her, yes, she would have been.

But what he had done to their daughters...

Had his attitudes shown up in the way he treated them? Had they already known how he felt?

Probably. Kids weren't stupid.

Adults were.

The office was a buzz of activity.

Set in the back corner of a two-story strip mall from the 1960s, Kwindale Investigations took up two-thirds of the lower L. The entry was behind some badly placed stairs. She could have moved the entry to another part of the L, but she didn't. She liked to make the clients work a bit before they hired her.

Three cars were in the parking lot when she pulled in, and all three belonged to her employees. She walked through the front, laptop under her arm. She had spent an inordinate amount of time cleaning herself up—changing out of the jeans and denim shirt, and opting for khakis and a white summer sweater instead.

She wasn't going to look like death warmed over anymore, not for the asshole she had married.

She was aware that the bitterness she felt was, in part, from the emails. The sender had achieved his goal in that, at least. But not all of it. If she hadn't already been toying with leaving Rob, she would have been a lot more confused, maybe even spiraling deeper into some kind of depression.

Right at the moment, though, depression seemed very far away. What she wanted was to mutilate her husband's corpse and castrate the person who had sent the grief spam to her daughters.

Why she thought the perpetrator was male, she had no idea, but she was convinced of it. And her hunches were almost never wrong.

The office seemed blessedly normal. The windows to the street were shaded, but the reception area was brightly lit thanks to the three sunlamps that her receptionist kept around the desk.

Smaller offices opened off this bigger room, and directly behind the reception area was a conference room with a long Formica table. Usually the table was filled with employees working off company laptops, but occasionally Lucca cleared it for a gigantic meeting with clients.

The office smelled of fresh oranges, which meant it was around 2 in the afternoon—exactly when Cornelius, her very first hire and now her right hand, had his mid-afternoon snack.

Lucca waved at the receptionist who started to ask how she was. Lucca pretended she didn't hear, opened the door to Cornelius's office without asking, and stepped inside.

He was a big man with a close-cropped afro. He favored loose clothing—today's shirt was a white-and-tan weave that looked like expensive "local" sourced material, just the kind of politically correct clothing he preferred. His gym bag was half open against the far wall, some sweat-stained clothes hanging out of it.

He stood as she came in.

"Lucca," he said in his deep George-accented voice. "I didn't expect you."

"Said I might be in today." She set the laptop on his desk.

"Yeah, but when you didn't return my call earlier, I figured you weren't coming." He frowned down at the laptop.

"I didn't even listen to the message," she said. "I need you on a case."

His eyes narrowed. She never said things like that—not anymore. Now, he brought in his own cases, just like she did.

"That's your computer," he said.

She nodded. It hadn't taken much for him to deduce that. She had stickers across the top of the laptop marking it as *Property of Lucca*. She had learned that the hard way, when she had accidentally opened a client's laptop thinking it was hers.

"The girls and I are being targeted by a spammer," she said. "I need you to find out who it is. I also need you to look at the photos in the early emails and see if they're just generic internet images, blurred, or if they're actually what they purport to be."

Cornelius slid the laptop to his side of the desk, then rested his fingertips on top of it.

"About that, Lucca," he said.

She frowned. "About what, exactly? I need you on the job. I don't want anyone else to see this—"

"No," he said. "About the spammer."

His expression was serious. He paused just long enough for her breath to catch.

"You got some spam too," she said.

"No," he said, "actually, we didn't. But the school district called. They got quite a bit, and they wanted us—they wanted me, specifically—to see if it was legit."

Lucca's cheeks heated. "Spam about Rob?"

Cornelius nodded.

"In email?" she asked.

He nodded again.

"When did it start showing up?" she asked.

"Right after he died," Cornelius said. "That morning, in fact."

She frowned. She hadn't expected that. The school district had gotten email before she had, which changed the focus of everything.

"What kind of email?" she asked.

"To tell the truth about Rob," Cornelius said.

"Pictures of affairs, and child abuse, and screen shots from chat rooms?"

Cornelius actually leaned back just a little. His face didn't register surprise, but his body did.

"No," he said. "Financial records."

She blinked, unprepared for that. "What kind of financial records?"

"The hacked kind," Cornelius said. "Rob's financial records."

"And mine?" she asked.

Cornelius shook his head. "Just his, from one local bank and two online banks."

"Online banks?" she asked. "We don't bank at online banks."

"I know," Cornelius said quietly. Everyone who worked at Kwindale Investigations knew what she thought of online bank security for some of those new start-up banks.

Rob had known that too.

"Rob had accounts of his own?" she asked.

Cornelius nodded again. It was almost as if he wanted her to make some kind of leap on her own.

"With what money?" she asked. "His paycheck was direct deposited into our joint account."

"He started the accounts with the school district's money," Cornelius said softly.

It took her a moment to connect the dots. Five years ago, Rob had been temporary treasurer for the school district when the original treasurer had been fired for cause. Rob had repaired the books, and had gotten them ready for a forensic accountant. Or so he said.

"Rob was the one embezzling?" Lucca asked. "Not that woman who got fired?"

"Oh, they both were, just at different times." Cornelius's fingers tapped Lucca's laptop. "He just took her ideas and improved on them."

For the second time that day, Lucca's knees gave out. She sat in the closest chair, a wooden thing without a cushion at all.

"And no one noticed money was still disappearing?" she asked.

"A lot of money went missing the first time," Cornelius said. "Or rather, Rob's reports said a lot of money went missing. He postulated there was one account that still had school district funds draining into it, but no one could find the fund."

"Because it was his," she said.

Cornelius didn't even bother to nod this time. He just watched her as if he expected her to burst into tears.

She was long past tears. She was long past anger. She had moved into an emotional space she had never occupied before. It was a kind of calm that felt powerful, as if it had a lot of energy behind it.

"How long have you been working on this?" she asked.

"Long enough to know I needed to notify you before you met with an attorney to help you with Rob's estate," Cornelius said.

She hadn't yet found an attorney. There had been no hurry because, under state law, everything passed directly to her. She had wanted to use Rob's death to put her own finances in order, to make sure the girls were cared for in a way that *she* wanted, not the ways that Rob had suggested.

The bastard.

Lucca let out a breath. When she had gone to an attorney and done a search of everything, she would have found these accounts. If she had waited a long time, it might have been hard to prove she hadn't known about them.

Embezzling. She hadn't expected it. But then, she hadn't expected any of this.

"How much are we talking?" Lucca asked, surprised her voice sounded as calm as it did.

"Enough that it puts him into the WTF category," Cornelius said.

It worried her that he didn't give her an amount. Although she had an idea from what he said. The WTF category was one they used in the office for the truly stupid, usually spouses who cheated on their partners and were blatant about it.

But with financial crimes, the WTF category was even more what-the-fuck. Kwindale Investigations (particularly Lucca and Cornelius) saved WTF on financial crimes for the person who had stolen or embezzled a boatload of money, and should have shipped the funds to one of those banks that kept no records, and then the person should have run off to a country with no extradition.

Doing it this way was just a guarantee that the person would eventually be caught.

Lucca rubbed a hand over her face, thinking about it all, thinking about Rob, wondering why he had become that man.

She had no answers.

"You're sure he did this," she said.

Cornelius nodded. "Our lovely hacker sent hundreds of emails of your husband in the one bank, and we could focus down on some of the forms he was filling out. He had the right account numbers."

Hundreds of emails. Lucca and the girls only had a few.

Lucca didn't say anything. She was trying to get her brain to function faster, but it was still stuck in grief mode.

"We've had two weeks to investigate this, Lucca," Cornelius said gently. "We're sure it was him."

She nodded. She had only had hours to investigate the grief spam she had received, and she was certain that the most harmful posts had been his as well.

"Do you know who is doing this?" she asked.

Cornelius sat down at his desk, putting it between him and her. He used to put furniture between them when he was a new hire, afraid she would get angry at him.

She never got that kind of angry, although she often made him redo a lot of his work, back in those days.

He was so far past redoing anything, so far past needing supervision, that she trusted every word he had said.

Of course, she had trusted Rob too—or had she? She had handled the family finances for years. Rob had been on a budget that they both set. She had kept to her budget too, except for her business. And all of the money she had earned at her business had gone back into her accounts.

He couldn't touch it.

Her famous hunches—she hadn't been paying attention to them when it came to her husband.

But to be fair to herself, he had been grandfathered in. He had been around before her hunches were something she trusted.

What had she said once about a client? That the woman had been a frog in a pan of cold water. The frog hadn't noticed that the water was heating up, until it was too late.

She had been that goddamn frog. How had she become that goddamn frog?

"Lucca?" Cornelius said.

She blinked, realizing he had been talking and she hadn't heard him.

"I'm sorry," she said. "Tell me again."

He bit his lower lip. "We've been focused on the embezzlement."

He didn't say anything more. He had been saying more when he had spoken the first time.

But he didn't need to say more. The client was the school district, and the school district had just discovered a major crime. Who had alerted them to that crime mattered less than the crime itself.

Lucca reached for the laptop. "You've got your hands full," she said. "I'll take care of this."

Cornelius's fingertips still rested on the silver surface, near Lucca's name.

"No," he said. "We have the resources here. We'll take care of it."

"I'm not sitting at home anymore," she said.

He frowned at her, then sighed. "Take care of the girls," he said.

"I will," she said. "And one way I will is to shut this asshole down."

Cornelius nodded. "I agree. That's important," he said. "But you can't be involved in this."

"I'm not a victim," Lucca said. "I can do this."

"But, Lucca," Cornelius said gently. "You are."

That rage she had been sitting on engulfed her. It took all of her strength to block the next words out of her mouth.

I am not, she would have said to him. *I am clearheaded and ready to work. I need to work. I need to catch this guy. I need to feel...*

Useful.

The word caught her, defused the rage, and made her tear up.

Cornelius didn't see the fight she was having internally. He was saying, "We're going to have to go to court and give testimony on this case, since we found the embezzlement thanks to this guy. We can't have you in the middle of all of that, Lucca. You're going to have to deal with the legal ramifications. These crimes have had an impact on you, whether you want to acknowledge that or not."

The crimes have had an impact on you. The words she had designed to convince victims who hated the word to accept that someone had hurt them.

"What can I do?" she asked.

"Let us track him down," Cornelius said. "And then we'll figure that out."

After Lucca left Cornelius, she went to her private office. It was neater than her home office. The desk was empty except for her computer, and the files she'd been working on—the paper files—were nowhere to be seen.

She had abandoned a dozen investigations in progress when Rob died, and she hadn't given them a second thought until now. Cornelius had clearly stepped in and taken over. She opened the computer, saw that he had assigned the cases that were nearly finished to the newest investigators, and gave the rest to the more experienced investigators.

Normally, he probably would have kept one or two for himself, but he hadn't, which told her how all-encompassing this investigation for the school district had been.

She sat down, and rubbed a hand over her face. She was tired. Not physically tired. Emotionally tired. She'd probably experienced every negative emotion possible so far today, and she would probably experience a few more before the day was out.

Starting with the emotions that were coming in the next few minutes.

She texted her daughters jointly and asked if she could set up a video conference. She would rather be discussing all of this with them in person, but everyone lived in different cities.

She had already toyed with the idea of telling the girls what she had learned later, when the investigations were done, but that would leave them with the uncertainty and the pain of those posts Rob had completed.

Better to rip off the Band-Aid quickly, as she had learned in her first few years of mothering. Sparing a child pain by not telling her something, or by telling it slowly, usually compounded the pain.

And this pain—thank you, Rob, you asshole—was impossible to ignore.

The girls were all available now for a video conference, and she braced herself. The last thing she wanted to do was tell her daughters that everything was true, and that there were even worse accusations.

But she was going to.

The call went through, and one by one, her daughters appeared on her computer screen. Marla had her curly hair pulled back, her face gray, and the shadows under her eyes deep. She looked like she hadn't slept in days.

Sybil wore a black blazer that accented her broad shoulders. A gold cross glinted on the Peter Pan collar of her black blouse. The color suited her, and gave her cheeks color, but her eyes resembled Marla's—sunken and haunted.

Antoinette's short black hair hadn't even been combed that day, or if her hair had been, she had run her fingers through it so many times it stuck out haphazardly around her face. Surprisingly, though, her eyes were dry. In them, Lucca saw a reflection of her own. Antoinette's voice hadn't shaken with unshed tears this morning; it had shaken with complete fury.

Lucca had forgotten that side of her youngest: when Antoinette got hurt, she rose up in righteous wrath, ready to do battle. She had even done so that day long ago when she'd broken her leg. Lucca had had to stop Antoinette from hitting the tree with her tiny little fists.

"It's true," Antoinette said tightly before anyone else could even say hello. "All of it. It's true."

"I don't know about all of it," Lucca said. She fell into a tone that she hadn't used in years—Reasonable Mom Voice. It said *This is awful, but I'm going to be calm, so you be calm too.* "But the screenshots, from what I can tell, they were written by your dad."

The girls all started talking at once. Angry, vengeful, tear-filled, horrified. And then Sybil burst into shaking gulping sobs, and all three of the others tried to comfort her from far away.

It was at that point that Lucca realized this wasn't a one phone call kinda thing. She was going to have to work with her girls on this horrid mess Rob had left them with every single day, maybe more than once.

Cornelius had been right: she was too close emotionally to do any of the fine computer work. Her computer work was going to have to be with her daughters, her friends, her colleagues—everyone who had known Rob, or thought they had.

Aren't you happy to be rid of that asshole now? The final email—all of the final emails—had read. *You really should thank me.*

Thank me.

As she talked to her daughters, as she listened to their pain, those last two words rolled around in her mind.

She wasn't going to thank whoever did this when she found out who it was. She really was going to eviscerate that person. Because her daughters hadn't needed to know any of this about their father. They could have blithely continued with their lives, feeling ambivalent about him, as Antoinette was saying right now ("I kinda knew he didn't like my choices, but I didn't realize...").

The jerk who had done this had taken any delusions her daughters had had away from them. And he wanted *credit*.

Which meant he wanted to be caught.

Something niggled in her mind at that.

"Mom?" Marla said. "You okay? Mom?"

Lucca blinked, focused, saw all of her daughters looking at their cameras, trying to see through their screens into hers. She wondered what she looked like. Probably as discombobulated as they did.

"No," she said. "I'm not okay. But I'm better than I was yesterday. I have a mission now. I'm going to figure this out for all of us."

When she was done with this call, though, she'd call each of her daughters individually, see if they needed her to come visit. Because she had broad shoulders, just like Sybil. Besides, part of her had divorced Rob emotionally years ago.

The girls were dealing with the loss of their father in two ways: they were dealing with his physical loss, and the loss of the man they had thought they knew.

Aren't you happy to be rid of that asshole now? You really should thank me.

Those words...

Lucca's brain caught the thought that had been niggling, held it, and let her examine it.

This guy, he was bragging. Not about the revelation.

About getting rid of Rob.

"Mom?" Sybil asked, her question sharp. "What are you thinking?"

Lucca made herself smile, knowing the smile was bitter and ironic, and not entirely caring.

"Oh, honey," she said in that Mom voice. "You really don't want to know."

When the most painful call of her life was finally over, Lucca stood. She was shaking. She had been emotionally drained before the call, and the conversation hadn't helped that—or the guilt. She should have seen what her husband had become.

Or maybe she should have seen what he was.

She could make all the excuses she wanted, but she was a woman who had prided herself on her ability to read people, and the one person in her life that she was (in theory) closest to was the one she had misread completely.

Which made her question whether or not she had misread others along the way.

She made herself take a deep breath. Now was not the time to doubt herself. She needed to be strong, for the girls—and for herself. She needed to figure out what happened.

She shut down the computer, then paced the small space between the desk and the door.

The police had assumed that Rob had been in a single-car crash. He was a respected high school principal, slightly tubby, middle-aged, a perfect candidate for a heart attack while driving or for a stroke. He might have fallen asleep at the wheel, the police officer who had called her had said, or maybe he had simply missed the corner in the dark.

Nothing unusual in their line of work, or so the police thought.

Because they hadn't known about the double life, about the embezzlement. About the person who had been watching and photographing Rob. Or who had been stealing photographs from security cameras.

The police hadn't known any of that, so they had no reason to investigate the matter further.

You really should thank me.

She owned the car now, or what was left of it. The impound had left a message on her phone a few days ago, asking if she wanted to claim the car. She only had a week or so, they said, to remove any belongings from the trunk or the back seat of the car. If the impound yard had left her that message, that meant there had been items left in the car.

Items that might give her a clue to Rob.

Or to the hacker, the stalker, or whoever he was.

She grabbed her purse, and let herself out of her office, waggling her fingers at Cornelius as she passed his office on the way to the main door.

He frowned at her, mouthed *Are you okay?* She nodded her

answer, then let herself outside, stopping for a moment in the bright sunshine.

It seemed incongruous, that sunshine—the opposite of the way she felt. It was a mocking sunshine, rather like the sunshine on 9/11 in New York. The kind of day that should have been perfect, if not for the plume of smoke trailing into the blue, blue sky.

Then Lucca shook her head. Rob had been dead sixteen days. The 9/11 analogy belonged to Day One, not Day Sixteen. By Day Sixteen, she should have been firmly inside the new reality of life without Rob.

Only Day Sixteen had turned into a brand-new Day One, the day in which she discovered that she had spent decades living a lie.

You really should thank me.

She got into her van, backed out of the small parking area, and drove as carefully as she could to the police impound yard at the north end of Watersville.

She had been to the impound yard dozens, if not hundreds, of times before, always on a case, always looking for whatever it was that someone had left behind.

Like she had almost left things behind. She would have, if she hadn't discovered Rob's perfidy. If the grief spam hadn't tilted her in the right direction.

Although it really wasn't fair to call what she had received grief spam. That had been the casket offers, the avoid-estate-tax directives, and the invest-your-inheritance scams. What she had gotten— what everyone who had been close to Rob had received—had been wake-up emails of a kind that was, in many ways, much worse than the grief spam. Grief spam was impersonal, at least.

This stuff...

She shook it off, trying not to think about her daughters' faces as she had seen them that afternoon. Lucca would look over Rob's car, get her belongings, and if she found nothing, go home.

The impound yard was in the bottom of a hollow about one-hundred yards from the entrance to the dump. During the wettest springs, the impound yard flooded thanks to the intersection of crisscrossing rivers that had given Watersville its name.

Behind the impound yard's chain-link fence, twenty or so cars had been stored as closely together as possible. They were the cars that had been towed here because they were parked illegally or because they had been booted and then abandoned. About half of those cars would get claimed every day, and the rest would eventually get resold at the police department auction.

Behind them, a squat brown building stood. It had enough room for two city employees, one tougher than the other because people sometimes got violent over their cars.

The damaged and destroyed cars, the cars that might be evidence in an actual crime, and the cars that had been stolen (and unclaimed) covered the vast brown dirt between the impound yard and the city dump. She knew from personal experience that some of those cars had sat on the dirt for years, waiting for someone to make a decision about their disposal.

She couldn't see Rob's pride and joy, the stupid red Camaro he had bought without telling her, so soon after Antoinette left for college. They had fought over that stupid car, because Lucca had believed they couldn't afford it. He said he would handle the payment himself, using the money he had out of the family budget for his own discretionary spending.

Since he had done that, she hadn't thought about the damn car again. But now that she knew about Rob's extra accounts, she figured that was what he had been using to pay for the stupid Camaro.

Lucca pulled open the door to the brown building, saw one of the employees—Stu—sitting behind the ancient desk. He stood when he saw her. He was wearing a white T-shirt with a band logo on it, the ridiculous green shirt the city made him wear draped over a chair.

"Hey, Lucca," he said gently. "Sorry about Rob."

She nodded, unwilling to acknowledge that sentence given the mood she was in.

"I hope you're here on a case," Stu said in that same tone.

"You guys called, said there were personal items in the Camaro."

She sounded normal—at least, she thought she sounded normal.

"Yeah," Stu said. "I can get them for you. You don't need to see that car."

"Actually," she said, "I do need to see the car."

"Honey," Stu said, "you really don't."

He had never called her "honey" before. The "honey" this time wasn't condescending, just affectionate. His lower lip was turned down a bit, and a frown creased his forehead.

Lucca wasn't going to tell him about the emails or the embezzlement or her suspicions. But she did need to ask him a few questions.

"You ever lose somebody close to you, Stu?" she asked.

"My mom." His frown grew deeper. "Two years ago."

"Then you know how it is," Lucca said. "Sometimes you get an idea in your head and you have to do what you can to get it out of your head."

He took a deep breath, clearly not sure what she was referring to. But she had united them in grief, and that had somehow made him willing to listen.

"The car look unusual to you?" she asked.

His lips got even thinner, as if he were holding back his words. After a pause that was seconds too long, he said, "It was totaled, Lucca, and the interior..."

"I know," she said, although she didn't, exactly. But she had dug through cars whose owners had died inside, sometimes in accidents, and in two instances by gunshot, and she knew that interiors were often filled with blood and brains.

"It's been in the sun," he said.

"I figured," she said.

"You don't need to—"

"Please, Stu," she said. "Answer me. Does the car look unusual to you?"

He closed his eyes as if willing her to go away. But she wasn't going to.

"The dents are wrong," he said, as if she had tortured the phrase out of him. "The back dents. They're all wrong."

He led her to the car—he insisted, and she wasn't going to argue.

The Camaro had been dumped in front of a group of cars that were almost unrecognizable as vehicles. They were twisted hunks of black and silver metal, accented by flat tires, popped hoods, and dented car doors. At least the Camaro looked like a car. A ruined car, but a car all the same.

The front end of the Camaro formed an uneven U. The bottom of the U still held the shape of that concrete barrier. She recognized it, had driven by it a million times before Rob's accident, and had always thought of the barrier as a hazard. She hadn't driven by the barrier since, because she knew the Camaro's silver paint would still be scraped along the edges.

She really hadn't expected to see that the Camaro had hugged the barrier. They probably had to use some special equipment to peel it away.

"Did they use the Jaws of Life?" she asked Stu.

He was staring at the vehicle as if it had harmed him personally. "No," he said. "The car wasn't hard to remove. The tires remained intact, so they could just pull it backwards. There've been so many accidents, the tow-truck drivers know how to get vehicles away from that barrier now."

Then he glanced at her to see if that sentence had offended her. It hadn't. Truth rarely offended. It was the lies that hurt.

That thought made her think of her daughters' faces, and tears threatened.

Stu put a hand on her arm. "I told you, this isn't a good idea."

Lucca willed the tears back. "Show me the dents."

As if there weren't enough dents. As if the car wasn't completely destroyed.

He gestured, but her eyes didn't follow quickly enough. They were still riveted to the front of the Camaro, to the windshield, which had bent with the frame, but hadn't shattered. It had spider-webbed instead, and Rob's blood decorated the cracks—black now with two weeks' worth of sunshine and decay.

That thought calmed her. He was gone. He was really and truly gone. Yes, he was still hurting them, but his actions were in the past. They were finite. Once she found out everything he did, she would be able to deal with it.

And, more importantly, she would be able to figure out how to help her daughters deal with it.

Stu looked at Lucca, clearly giving her a moment. "You still want to see it?"

"Sorry," she said.

He gestured again, and this time she watched. She still didn't see what he was gesturing at.

"Just take me over there," she said, and hoped she didn't sound exasperated.

He walked cautiously across the dirt, then crouched beside the Camaro.

"Here," he said, his hand above several deep scrapes on the rear driver's side. "And here." He moved a little closer to the rear bumper.

Rob had bought a black bumper cover for both bumpers, so they "added to the classiness of the vehicle" or so he said. She thought they made little difference.

The bumper cover was torn in three places now because the bumper itself was dented, with small V-shaped dents, spaced oddly along its length.

Rob had been protective of this car. He had come home one afternoon bitching that someone had opened a door and made a dime-sized groove near the gas tank.

He would never have allowed something like these dents.

"You think this happened at the same time?" she asked.

Stu shrugged. "I don't know about the timing of these, or the one on the driver's side," he said. "But look at this."

He moved to the passenger side of the car, and pointed to the rear bumper there.

It took her a moment to realize that the cover remained, hanging by its edges, but the bumper itself was so crumpled that it almost looked flat. It was also silver and blue, which struck her as odd.

She looked over at Stu. He was frowning.

"Think about this." He pointed at the damage in the back. "Here." Then he pointed at the gigantic U in the front of the vehicle. "And there."

She stepped back so she could see both together.

"The bumper stuff wasn't tow-truck damage?" she asked.

"They didn't attach to the bumper," he said. "They put the car on a flatbed."

"Oh." She swallowed. If she had hit the Camaro in that exact spot with a lot of force on the road not too far from the concrete barrier, she could have sent the Camaro into the barrier, in just that way. Rob wouldn't have had time to correct.

She had thought of that scenario often on that bit of road, especially when someone had been tailgating her. She had known just how easy it would have been to get accidentally shoved into that barrier, which was why so many people had been injured there.

"You're saying this was deliberate?" she asked.

"If I were the investigating officer, I'd take a look," Stu said. "The same paint is on both sides and the back end of the car. Had your husband been in an accident with the vehicle before this?"

"No," she said. She had seen the car the morning before the accident. The Camaro's red paint had glistened in the early morning sunlight as Rob had driven off to school—or at least, that was where she had thought he was going. Now, she wasn't sure. Then, she had thought like she had every morning, that Rob was stupid to take his expensive midlife crisis and park it in a spot marked Principal, putting a gigantic target on his toy.

"So this was all new," Stu said.

"Yeah," she said.

"Then someone kept hitting him," Stu said.

"You think they forced him into the barrier?" she asked.

"Dunno that. It would take a crash scene investigator to know for sure and it might be too late to do a great examination. But if your husband was speeding to get away from someone, then looked over his shoulder, and didn't realize quite where he was, he could have driven into that barrier. And honestly, given the way the Camaro's built, he would have had to have been going really fast—way over the speed limit—to do that kind of damage to the vehicle."

She walked around the Camaro. She couldn't quite get to the front, which was fine. The windows on both the passenger and driver's side had cracked from the impact, but not as badly. The rear window was just fine.

But the sides were scraped, and the back was badly damaged. Stu was right; someone had definitely hit this car more than once. And the car wasn't rear-ended the way a car would have been had someone hit it after the accident with the barrier. Then the car would have accordioned. It hadn't.

"Did you tell the police?" Lucca had a hunch she knew the answer, but she asked anyway.

"They had already closed the investigation when they brought the car here," Stu said.

Which was why he could call her and tell her to pick up Rob's things.

"But you could have called them when you saw the damage," she said.

He opened his hands, as if to say *What can I do?* "I had no idea if the damage predated the final accident. I see a lot of stuff, Lucca."

She knew that. Which was why she had trusted him in numerous investigations. He saw things, but he was cautious.

She opened her purse, and rummaged around until she found one of her evidence bags. She pulled it out, along with a small scraper she had bought just for this kind of thing.

Then she walked over to one of the dents, crouched, and scraped some of the blue paint into the bag.

"Lucca," Stu said in a chiding tone. "Tampering with evidence."

"Evidence of what?" she asked. "At this moment, there's no case. And besides, the car's been sitting in the lot for more than two weeks. Anyone could have done this."

"You shouldn't be investigating," Stu said. "He was your husband."

The second person that day to warn her off an investigation. She would have paid attention too, if she had planned to bring charges. But she was just trying to figure out what had happened.

"Call the police when I leave," she said. "Please tell them I had said the car was undamaged the moment of the accident and—"

"And I got a twinge of conscience and felt they should reopen the investigation." He nodded. They had done this dance a few times before, but never on something so personal. "Sure thing, Lucca. As long as you're sure you want this."

Her gaze met his. His blue eyes were clear, but that frown remained.

Did he know something about Rob that she didn't? Oh, hell. Everyone probably knew something about Rob that she didn't.

"Yes," she said. "I want this. I want this very much."

And within the hour, she was back in the inner sanctum. Back when she started as a private detective, she did a lot of work for insurance companies. Often that involved identifying cars from hit-and-run accidents. She had learned a lot of short cuts to identifying paint chips, shortcuts that didn't involve a mass spectrometer or a chromograph.

She had learned long ago that the big forensic science stuff wasn't always necessary. Sometimes she just needed common sense—and the ability to hack into the police department records.

First thing she did was look at stolen car reports for that week in April, isolating blue cars only. She found six cars stolen, and only two had a shade of blue even close to the one she was looking at.

One of those cars had been found. It had been totaled. The police figured someone had taken it on a joyride.

She figured someone had used it to repeatedly slam into Rob's car.

GRIEF SPAM

Then she leaned back and stared at the car itself. It was a 2017 sports car with enough horsepower to go after a Camaro, and enough weight to do some damage.

The police report said the interior of the sports car had been wiped clean, which was unusual in a joyride. Usually the joyrider figured that the car was so damaged no one would dust for prints. And usually, the joyrider would be right.

Then she went back to the police report. The car was reported stolen at seven the morning Rob was killed. Four hours after he died.

Police discovered the car two days later at the bottom of an empty culvert about fifteen blocks from where the sports car had supposedly been stolen.

The car's owner lived nowhere near either place. He lived on the south side of Watersville, in one of the many apartment complexes that littered the freeway.

Yet he had called, saying he had come out in the morning to find the car missing. How could he have come out in the morning from his apartment to find the car missing from a completely different address?

The details didn't entirely add up.

She looked at the owner's name. The car was registered in the name of Thomas G. Hedges. Hedges. That name rang a bell.

Thomas Hedges. Tom Hedges. Tommy Hedges.

Yes, indeed. Tommy Hedges. He had gone to Anderson High School. His family had moved to Watersville the year before—something about a high-end divorce. His mother had moved the children to a small town to give them "real life." But Tommy had acted out, and Rob had finally expelled him.

Rob had been obsessed with the entire thing, because the mother had called the school board. It had all escalated and someone—Lucca couldn't remember who—finally took the mother aside and told her to send the boy to some rich kid's boarding school.

Lucca had gone to one of the school board meetings during all of that, and she remembered the mother—too thin and dressed to the nines, an aging trophy wife who had been replaced by another trophy

—sobbing, begging the school board to let her boy back in, saying he needed to learn how everyone else lived more than he needed to have a high-end education, despite his computer skills.

That had caught Lucca's attention, because she'd sat through a number of those meetings before, usually as Rob's support, sometimes for clients, and no one had said the quality of the education didn't matter. They had always been urging the Watersville School District to up its game, not implying that its sheer ordinariness was a plus.

But did Lucca remember this right? Had the mother actually said *Despite his computer skills?* Or had Lucca heard that elsewhere?

She moved to a different laptop to search for everything she could find on Tommy Hedges. She felt she had to move to a clean laptop just in case he did have mad computer skills.

Just in case he was the person she was looking for.

He had an online presence—everyone did, so that was no surprise. His Facebook page had been active years ago, but he rarely posted now. He did post images of his apartment a few months ago —a one-bedroom cookie cutter, remodeled a little, but its 1970s roots still showed.

Such a comedown, he wrote. *See what happens when you have to pay for shit yourself?*

His other social media accounts were just as sketchy until she stumbled on his second Twitter handle. It was FormerRichBoy1994, and the invective in it was startling. He wasn't nasty like Rob had been. Tommy Hedges didn't write nasty things about people of color or women or engage in any of those online hatred memes.

Instead, he called out hypocrisy, and blamed the system for robbing him of his life. He hadn't Tweeted much recently, but the day after Rob died, he Tweeted: *No one gets it. They think he's a goddamn saint.*

And then a day later: *I think I did this all wrong. I think if I don't get recognition, it will destroy me.*

She wondered if it was a confession, or if it had nothing to do with Rob at all, if she was making it all up.

GRIEF SPAM

She took her hands off the keys and shut the laptop. Stu's and Cornelius's caution had been right: she wanted someone to be guilty —not of killing Rob, but of hurting her daughters.

Lucca wanted to go after whoever it was so badly she had felt something new within herself: she had felt the willingness to blame someone else, based on almost no evidence at all.

She stood up, took the laptop, and placed it in the closet. Then she walked out of the inner sanctum into the messy outer sanctum.

Once there, she pulled her cell phone out of her pocket and called Cornelius.

"I think I have something for you to look into," she said. "And I think you'd better do it now."

After that, things moved both faster and slower than she expected.

Faster: the speed of the investigation into the car. Stu's phone call got the police involved, and since Rob had been well liked, the police decided to take another look.

They found all the discrepancies she found. The physical evidence was nearly overwhelming—all of it, scrapes and paint chips and a direct line from Tommy Hedges to Rob.

Tommy Hedges blamed Rob for everything bad that had happened to him after getting expelled from school. The police found other fake identities, other postings, and could link the young man to Rob's murder with startling ease. There was even traffic camera footage that showed the blue car trailing the Camaro. No footage of the actual hits with the car—clearly Hedges had been too smart for that—but there was enough to make a case against him.

Slower than expected: the embezzlement case against Rob. It looked like the school district would just take the money back, without getting too deep into the mess. Lucca wouldn't face charges, because it was pretty clear she knew nothing about any of it.

And while she found that embarrassing, it was also a relief.

Everything else seemed out of time. Her reactions were slower or swifter, depending. Her conversations with her daughters were awkward and sad.

She tried to book a trip to see Antoinette, but Antoinette claimed she was doing all right—that she had help—and recommended that she see Sybil.

Sybil said her church was helping, and Lucca's presence would just remind her of everything she didn't want to think about.

Marla said she had a therapist, and they were working on it one day at a time. But if Lucca felt like she needed comfort, then she was welcome to come visit.

Lucca wasn't sure she did need comfort. She wasn't sure what she needed.

She still cried too much, but she was no longer certain what she was crying about.

She had to break out of this funk. She was beginning to think the tears were coming from unexpressed anger—anger at Rob for leaving her with such a mess, for lying, for being a true bastard. And anger at Tommy Hedges for shattering her family with his horrid grief spam.

She couldn't do anything about her anger at Rob, but she could do something about her anger at Tommy.

It would just take a little time to arrange.

He was in county jail, because he didn't have enough money for bail and his mother refused to bail him out. But she had provided an expensive lawyer, and they had a strategy, which meant Tommy was not talking to the police.

But Lucca thought he might talk to her.

She didn't ask permission from anyone. She knew it would be denied. The police would worry that she was going to screw up the case; the lawyer probably thought she would be acting on the police's behalf.

She was prepared for this meeting, emotionally and physically.

GRIEF SPAM

She knew what she could and couldn't get away with. She knew how to handle everything—even if Hedges tried to hurt her.

She had gone in and out of that jail more times than she could count, and the guards there gave her a lot of leeway. She had put away some of the worst criminals in Watersville. She had also gotten a few people out.

And she had always treated everyone who worked in the jail with respect, because she knew they had one of the harder jobs in the county.

The building was a squat 1970s cinderblock. She entered the way she always did, asked to see Hedges, and was told to wait. No one questioned her being there, no one asked her why she needed to see him. Just noted he hadn't gotten a lot of visitors.

Then she was cleared. She had to meet him in the main visitor's area. A family congregated near one of the bolted down tables on the far side of the room, the three children old enough to know where they were. They were looking around nervously, their parents talking quietly, the woman with her hand on the arm of the youngest as if afraid to let go.

Lucca took a table as far from them as she could get. She nodded at the two guards positioned nearest the doors, then waited.

It didn't take long for them to bring Hedges to her. He looked sallow in the orange short-sleeve jumpsuit, his hair cropped short, his skin blotchy. His gaze focused on her, and his eyes narrowed.

"You think I don't know who you are," he said as he sat down. "You're his wife. Lucca Kwindale."

No guard was close enough to overhear the conversation.

"You want to know why I killed him," Hedges said. "That's what everyone wants to know. Not *if* I killed him. *Why* I killed him."

His arms were flabby and surprisingly for someone of his age, without tattoos. She hadn't said a word so far, just watched him, and he seemed content with that.

"I'm not going to tell you anything about that night," he said. "My lawyer said I shouldn't talk to anyone."

He wanted her to ask why he was talking to her. He wanted her to feel special—look! I'm talking with you when I'm not supposed to—but she wasn't going to play that game.

"I don't care why you killed him," she said, her voice soft and low. "Believe me, I get it."

He raised his thin eyebrows. "You get it. You didn't get anything before. You're one of the dumbest bitches who ever walked. Or you're complicit in everything he did."

She thought she had been prepared for those sentiments, but she hadn't been. They stabbed, hard, because both statements were true.

But she had sat across from prisoners before—she had sat across from guilty people before—and she knew how to keep up the appearance of calm even when she wasn't.

"All I want to know," she said, "is why you sent the emails."

A tiny smile played at the corners of his mouth before he could get control of his face. "Some lawyer send you?"

She shook her head.

"Some prosecutor, to see if I'll talk?"

"If that were the case," she said, "we'd be in a different room, with more privacy, so that they could record everything."

"You probably have one of those tiny cameras on you," he said, arms crossed.

"I can't," she said. "I'm not authorized."

He made a face. She wasn't sure he believed her. He clearly weighed his choices for a moment: did he talk to her, risking a camera recording everything? Or did he walk away, and never find out why she was here?

She let him work it out. He had been obsessed with Rob. Rob was gone and she was all that was left. She was gambling that Hedges would choose to stay for that reason.

"So," Hedges said after a moment, and her heart did a little victory dance. "*You* want to know something."

"Why did you send those emails?" she asked.

"Bothered you, did they?" he asked.

"Yes," she said. "It makes no sense to me. You could have gotten away with everything if you hadn't sent the emails."

His crossed arms tightened, pulling on the jumpsuit. "Criminals are dumb," he said sullenly.

She quietly admired how he said that. He hadn't admitted any guilt at all.

"But you're not," she said. "What was the point? Rob was dead."

Hedges' eyes glittered. She recognized the rage in them; she'd seen it in her own eyes of late.

"He ruined my life," Hedges said so softly she could barely hear him over the echoey conversation across the room.

"I know," she said. "He expelled you from school and that started a spiral."

Hedges slammed his hands on the tabletop, making her jump. "It did *not*!" he shouted.

One of the guards came toward her, but she waved him off. The little family watched, the woman holding the youngest tightly against her as if Lucca had shouted at the little girl.

"That's what ruined you, right?" Lucca asked.

"*God*!" Hedges said. "Don't you *fucking* pay attention? Do I have to send more goddamn emails?"

His anger was a physical force. She could feel each word as if it were a punch.

"He didn't embezzle from you," she said.

"No," Hedges said. "He just fucked me."

"He fucked over everyone," she said.

"No," Hedges said again. "He *fucked* me."

His words rang in the concrete room. One of the children was crying. Now, Lucca wished they had taken the conversation elsewhere.

And she realized at that moment, she had deflected what Hedges was saying, tried not to hear it, would have set it somewhere else if she could.

"That second email," she said. "The images were generic."

"Because your goddamn husband was smart," Hedges said. "No contact in person, no pictures, no kiddie porn on his computer. Believe me, I looked."

Her heart started pounding.

"I had some pictures of my own, though," Hedges said. "Small camera, set up just right. But I kept looking at it. I. Kept. Looking at it. And he saw that, he found it, and *that's* when he expelled me. My mom thought I was acting out."

"You accused him?" Lucca said.

"Yeah," Hedges said. "No one listened. He was so fucking respected in this town."

Lucca's breath caught. That was why the police investigation into the accident moved so fast. They already had a police report from years ago linking Rob and Hedges, but it had been buried, possibly because Hedges was a juvenile, probably because Rob was the principal and above reproach.

Lucca swallowed, astounded at her own unwillingness to see her husband for who he was.

"No one told me," she said quietly.

And no one had even tried. She would have remembered.

"I know," Hedges said. "I found out later. The Old Boy Network buried the thing good and fast. They even convinced my mom I was a problem."

"She defended you," Lucca said, remembering the tearful school board meeting. "She tried to keep you here."

"Yeah, she thought that would be good for me. She thought I was making shit up because I was mad. *She* was the one who did that. She accused my dad of all kinds of crap he had never done." Hedges paused, took a deep breath, then narrowed his eyes. "Got your answers now?"

"No," Lucca said. She folded her arms and rested them on the tabletop. "I understand sending emails to the school board. I understand sending them to me. But to my daughters?"

That last word wobbled. She hadn't been able to hide her anger there.

"They're adults," he said.

"They loved him," Lucca said.

"Really?" he asked. "That asshole? Surely they knew what a jerk he was."

Maybe they had. And maybe they had been pretending, like Lucca had, that Rob was better than he was.

Sometimes losing the delusion was harder than losing the person.

"See?" Hedges said. "You should thank me."

"For what, exactly?" she asked.

His smile grew. "For all of it. For waking you up. For freeing you of him. For making sure he'll never hurt anyone again."

Hedges had just admitted to the murder. Her heart started pounding, hard, but she worked on keeping her expression neutral.

"Did he know it was you in the car?" she asked.

"He knew it was me for months," Hedges said. "Those emails didn't just come together after the fucker died, you know. He'd been getting them forever."

Rob had been getting more and more nervous. She hadn't really paid a lot of attention.

"What changed?" she asked.

Hedges eyes narrowed. "What do you mean?"

"Emails for months," she said. "And then, one night, you get in your car..."

Hedges laughed. "You don't know, do you? You really don't know."

Her cheeks warmed.

He touched one of his fingers to his own cheek, acknowledging her blush. "You don't know," he said with satisfaction. "He had just bought a condo in Perast."

"Where?" she asked before she could think the question through.

"Montenegro." Hedges' smile was wide. He was enjoying her ignorance. "No extradition."

She frowned. "But I didn't find any plane tickets."

"Because he was looking at charters," Hedges said. "That's how I caught him. Looking at charters. He had such a vast digital footprint. He had no idea I was onto that."

"You found it that night?" she asked, letting her own confusion into her voice. Her sorrow seemed to make him talkative.

"Just before I saw him at the restaurant. With one of the boys from the basketball team. The look on that kid's face—I sent the waiter over, told the kid there was an emergency at home, and then I watched while your husband left. He didn't see me until the first time I hit his car. I turned on the dome light, so he could see my face. And he looked scared."

Funny, she didn't care that Rob had been scared. She didn't care that he had died that night. She didn't care about him at all.

But their daughters—what this man had done—she wasn't going to let them come to a trial. And there would be a trial. Because Lucca had caught him.

He had asked about a camera, and she had lied. She hadn't told him she'd been wearing a small audio recorder disguised as one of the buttons on her collar.

She didn't tell him that. She didn't have to.

Prisoners in the county jail were not accorded the right to privacy unless they were meeting with their attorney, which he most decidedly was not.

She had thought she would feel more elated if she got him to confess.

Instead, she just felt dirty and sad.

"He hurt you," she said.

"Oh, yeah, that son of a bitch," Hedges said.

"But you're the one who has chosen to let that destroy you," she said.

His hands curled into fists. "I thought you might say something like that. I thought about that long and hard. Then I figured I could show you holier-than-thou assholes what it's like to have everything taken from you. I'd show you just how easy it is to get over events that totally destroy everything you've ever known."

She studied him for a minute. Then nodded. He was really smart. He could have chosen another way, no matter how difficult.

He hadn't.

And she saw no point in telling him that.

She stood, signaled the guard to let her out, and watched as the door swung back. She could leave. Hedges couldn't.

By his choice.

She had her answers. She also had a lot of soul searching to do. And daughters to help, in her own way.

She had some changes to make. She wasn't as good a detective as she had thought she was. She wasn't even as good a person as she had thought she was.

She needed to change all of that. And the first step was selling the business to Cornelius. Then she needed to do some work, some investigation—not of bad guys—but of the way people survived trauma like her daughters were going through. Like Hedges had gone through.

"You're just going to bury this, aren't you?" Hedges shouted after her. "Do you know how many lives he ruined?"

She stopped before stepping all the way out. She turned her head so she could just see him over her shoulder, still sitting at that table.

"Not yet," she said. "But I mean to find out."

And she would.

Rob wouldn't have been the kind of man who could handle reparations. But she could.

And she would do it.

She owed the community that much.

She owed her daughters even more.

Maybe she *should* thank Hedges. Because without the grief spam, she would never have known. And her daughters would have had to work out their daddy issues on their own.

Then Hedges smiled at her—a mean and feral smile. No. She wasn't going to thank him.

She wasn't in the mood to thank anyone.

She'd been angry for nearly three weeks now. She'd probably be angry for many, many more.

She would use that anger. Because now she had a focus.

All she needed now was a schedule.

Because schedules had value, Rob. Schedules defeated bad guys.

Even when they were already dead.

ABOUT THE EDITOR
Kristine Kathryn Rusch

New York Times bestselling author Kristine Kathryn Rusch writes in almost every genre. Generally, she uses her real name (Rusch) for most of her writing. Under that name, she publishes bestselling science fiction and fantasy, award-winning mysteries, acclaimed mainstream fiction, controversial nonfiction, and the occasional romance. Her novels have made bestseller lists around the world and her short fiction has appeared in eighteen best of the year collections. She has won more than twenty-five awards for her fiction, including the Hugo, *Le Prix Imaginales*, the *Asimov's* Readers Choice award, and the *Ellery Queen Mystery Magazine* Readers Choice Award.

Publications from *The Chicago Tribune* to *Booklist* have included her Kris Nelscott mystery novels in their top-ten-best mystery novels of the year. The Nelscott books have received nominations for almost every award in the mystery field, including the best novel Edgar Award, and the Shamus Award.

She writes goofy romance novels as award-winner Kristine Grayson.

She also edits. Beginning with work at the innovative publishing company, Pulphouse, followed by her award-winning tenure at *The Magazine of Fantasy & Science Fiction*, she took fifteen years off before returning to editing with the original anthology series *Fiction River,* published by WMG Publishing. She acts as series editor with her husband, writer Dean Wesley Smith.

To keep up with everything she does, go to kriswrites.com and sign up for her newsletter. To track her many pen names and series, see their individual websites (krisnelscott.com, kristinegrayson.com, retrievalartist.com, divingintothewreck.com, fictionriver.com, pulphousemagazine.com).

ALSO FROM WMG PUBLISHING

FICTION RIVER
Kristine Kathryn Rusch & Dean Wesley Smith, series editors

Doorways to Enchantment
Edited by Dayle A. Dermatis

Stolen
Edited by Leah Cutter

Chances
Edited by Kristine Grayson

Passions
Edited by Kristine Kathryn Rusch

Broken Dreams
Edited by Kristine Kathryn Rusch

Missed a previously published volume? No problem. Buy individual volumes anytime from your favorite bookseller.

Unnatural Worlds
Edited by Dean Wesley Smith & Kristine Kathryn Rusch

How to Save the World
Edited by John Helfers

Time Streams
Edited by Dean Wesley Smith

Christmas Ghosts
Edited by Kristine Grayson

Hex in the City
Edited by Kerrie L. Hughes

Moonscapes
Edited by Dean Wesley Smith

Special Edition: Crime
Edited by Kristine Kathryn Rusch

Fantasy Adrift
Edited by Kristine Kathryn Rusch

Universe Between
Edited by Dean Wesley Smith

Fantastic Detectives
Edited by Kristine Kathryn Rusch

Past Crime
Edited by Kristine Kathryn Rusch

Pulse Pounders
Edited by Kevin J. Anderson

Risk Takers
Edited by Dean Wesley Smith

Alchemy & Steam
Edited by Kerrie L. Hughes

Valor
Edited by Lee Allred

Recycled Pulp
Edited by John Helfers

Hidden in Crime
Edited by Kristine Kathryn Rusch

Sparks
Edited by Rebecca Moesta

Visions of the Apocalypse
Edited by John Helfers

Haunted
Edited by Kerrie L. Hughes

Last Stand
Edited by Dean Wesley Smith & Felicia Fredlund

Tavern Tales
Edited by Kerrie L. Hughes

No Humans Allowed
Edited by John Helfers

Editor's Choice
Edited by Mark Leslie

Pulse Pounders: Adrenaline
Edited by Kevin J. Anderson

Feel the Fear
Edited by Mark Leslie

Superpowers
Edited by Rebecca Moesta

Justice
Edited by Kristine Kathryn Rusch

Wishes
Edited by Rebecca Moesta

Pulse Pounders: Countdown
Edited by Kevin J. Anderson

Hard Choices
Edited by Dean Wesley Smith

Feel the Love
Edited by Mark Leslie

Special Edition: Spies
Edited by Kristine Kathryn Rusch

Special Edition: Summer Sizzles
Edited by Kristine Kathryn Rusch

Superstitious
Edited by Mark Leslie

FICTION RIVER PRESENTS
Allyson Longueira, Series Editor

Fiction River's line of reprint anthologies.

Fiction River has published more than 400 amazing stories by more than 100 talented authors since its inception, from *New York Times* bestsellers to debut authors. So, WMG Publishing decided to start bringing back some of the earlier stories in new compilations.

VOLUMES:
Debut Authors
The Unexpected
Darker Realms
Racing the Clock
Legacies
Readers' Choice
Writers Without Borders
Among the Stars
Sorcery & Steam
Cats!
Mysterious Women
Time Travelers

To learn more or to pick up your copy today, go to www.FictionRiver.com.

PULPHOUSE FICTION MAGAZINE

Pulphouse Fiction Magazine, edited by Dean Wesley Smith, made its return in 2018, twenty years after its last issue. Each new issue contains about 70,000 words of short fiction. This reincarnation mixes some of the stories from the old *Pulphouse* days with brand-new fiction. The magazine has an attitude, as did the first run. No genre limitations, but high-quality writing and strangeness.

For more information or to subscribe, go to www.pulphousemagazine.com.